Praise for

ELLA JONES *vs the* SUN STEALER

"A thrilling 8+ adventure with a gutsy,
determined protagonist"
Guardian

"A super adventure with a powerful
cast of characters"
The Sun, Book of the Week

"A blend of adventure, mystery and fantasy
with a brilliant and inspiring heroine"
Week Junior, Book of the Week

"A powerful story of resilience, offering young
readers a fast-paced journey full of courage"
School Reading List website

"High-stakes plot and compelling detail
makes for a gripping read"
BookTrust

Lucy Edwards is a blind broadcaster, content creator and disability activist who is usually accompanied by her guide dog Molly. At only seventeen, Lucy lost her eyesight due to a rare condition called incontinentia pigmenti, but her motto in life is that she is "blind, not broken". She took to YouTube and TikTok and started to upload her experiences, paving the way for change across the platforms. Several years later, Lucy became an ambassador for Pantene, featuring in their TV adverts, and for Mattel's recent far-reaching Blind Barbie press launch. Lucy continues to campaign for inclusivity, within the beauty industry and beyond.

NaviLens

NaviLens is an accessibility app specifically designed to help blind and partially sighted users explore independently around cities and their environment. By downloading the NaviLens app, users can detect their unique codes by simply pointing their phone in the direction of the code, allowing them to access all the information about that location or item audibly. You can use the NaviLens app on the cover to hear about the author, what the book is about and hear descriptions of the cover and pictures.

ELLA JONES *vs the* BATTLE NOISE

LUCY EDWARDS

with *Katy Birchall*

Illustrated by Luna Valentine

SCHOLASTIC

Published in the UK by Scholastic, 2025
Scholastic, Bosworth Avenue, Warwick, CV34 6UQ
Scholastic Ireland, 89E Lagan Road,
Dublin Industrial Estate, Glasnevin, Dublin, D11 HP5F

SCHOLASTIC and associated logos are trademarks and/or
registered trademarks of Scholastic Inc.

Written in collaboration with Katy Birchall
Text © Lucy Edwards, 2025
Inside illustrations by Luna Valentine © Scholastic, 2025

The moral rights of the author have been asserted by them.

ISBN 978 0702 33797 0

A CIP catalogue record for this book is available from the British Library.

Printed in the UK
Paper made from wood grown in sustainable forests
and other controlled sources.

MIX
Paper | Supporting
responsible forestry
FSC
www.fsc.org   FSC® C018072

1 3 5 7 9 10 8 6 4 2

www.scholastic.co.uk

For safety or quality concerns:
UK: www.scholastic.co.uk/productinformation
EU: www.scholastic.ie/productinformation

For my beautiful husband, Ollie.

Dearest Olga, my first-ever guide dog. You will forever be the light in my darkness.

PROLOGUE

When Everett Croft arrived at his office early one morning, he didn't expect a god to be there. But that's who he found waiting for him, looking out of the penthouse windows on the seventy-third floor of Croft Tower: a being so mighty and powerful that in his presence Everett's entire body trembled, fear coursing through his veins and turning his blood to ice.

"Wh-who are you?" Everett stammered in a croaked whisper, cowering back against his office door, his eyes widening as the god turned to face him.

The dark-haired god towered over Everett. He was impossibly tall and muscled, wearing worn, bronzed body armour that was damaged and dented. Scars covered the god's arms – old wounds left over from centuries of fighting battles and winning wars. At first glance, he was young and strikingly handsome, but as Everett continued staring the god's appearance warped and aged to that of an old man, his skin gaunt and wearied. Everett tried to tear his gaze away, disturbed by the god's changing appearance, but he found he could not. He was mesmerized by this being.

"Don't you recognize me, *Everett Croft*?" his visitor sneered, his low resounding voice echoing around the room, his eyes flashing blood-red. "You are an expert in the gods, are you not? That is what you pride yourself on being." He moved towards Everett, his stride so large he covered the entire office floor in just a few steps. "You have spent your life learning our stories, you've collected our things, and you have tried to bend us to your will."

Everett gulped at the god's venomous tone.

He was, of course, speaking the truth. Everett Croft was a successful entrepreneur and businessman who had made his multi-million-pound fortune in tech products and inventions, but he had also always been fascinated with deities and legend, dedicating hours and hours of research to all the different mythologies: Greek, Celtic, Norse, Egyptian,

Aztec – the list went on. As Everett became richer and more powerful, so his obsession intensified. Over the years, he had collected rare artefacts and documents believed to have mythological connections; he'd funded excavations and archaeological digs in the hunt for priceless treasures; he'd read and analysed every mythological book and theory that had ever been published in the hope that he might find a god who would be the key to unlocking his biggest obsession of all: to gain world power.

The truth was, Everett Croft wished for the impossible: that he could be a god himself.

He came excruciatingly close to achieving his goal just weeks earlier. After years of planning, he helped to free Lugh, a god who had been locked away by druids for centuries and who had vowed his vengeance on men by stealing the sun. In preparation for Lugh's plot, Everett had designed and produced the Croft Beacon, the only light source that would work in the eternal darkness Lugh had vowed to bring to the human race that had betrayed him.

It was a perfect, flawless plan and right on cue, every nation descended into chaos. For a while, things ticked along very nicely. World leaders clamoured for the Croft Beacons – the first product in Everett's extensively prepared line – all of them willing to pay a hefty price. Everett would have been rich beyond his wildest dreams, but more than that, he would have been worshipped and admired. The man who had brought back light to the world. A true hero. A god on earth.

But then…

Well, it all went wrong. Everything – the power, the money, the fame, the popularity – slipped from his grasp. No, it was *taken* from him. Taken by a little girl, who somehow managed to persuade Lugh that people were better than he thought and that they deserved light to be brought back to them. A little girl named Ella Jones.

And now he had sworn to get his revenge.

"I know that you tried to get Lugh to do your bidding," said the god in his office, jolting him from his vengeful thoughts about Ella.

"I … I merely tried to encourage Lugh to fulfil his destiny," Everett squeaked, cowering under the being's bone-chilling glower. "And if … if there's anything I can d-do for you … uh…"

He trailed off, desperately trying to work out who this god was before making any promises. His presence had made the room colder somehow, and his voice had made all the hairs on Everett's arms stand on end. His eyes were filled with anger and hatred. While Everett did not know his name, he could tell he was not here to make the world a happier place. Perhaps Everett could use that to his advantage.

"I am Homados," his unwelcome companion informed him at last.

"God of battle noise," Everett whispered in amazement, his eyes trailing over the symbols on Homados's tunic beneath the armour. "The personification of tumult and the din of war. It really is *you*. Wh-what do you want with me?"

"I'm looking for the Eye of Horus," Homados told him. "The pendant was once worn by Lugh, god of sun, light and justice. I've been searching for him for a long time in the hope of … *persuading* him to hand it over to me. I received word that he had escaped from prison and he was among the mortals here on earth, but I have now come to learn that I am too late. He has given the Eye of Horus away. I believe you know who has it."

Everett bowed his head as Homados glared at him, a shiver running down his spine.

"I … I do know," Everett whispered, his voice weak and wobbly.

"So, you will prove useful to me then." Homados lifted his chin in satisfaction. "I need it for the shield."

"The shield?" Everett cautiously lifted his head to check he'd heard correctly. "You're going after the Shield of Hercules."

"You know it," Homados said in a low, almost-impressed growl.

"I … I've read that, once completed with the Eye of Horus, it gives its wielder an extraordinary power of protection, making you … unbeatable against man and gods alike." Everett gulped. "Is that why you want it? Ultimate power over our world and … beyond?"

The lips of Homados slowly stretched into a smile so wicked that Everett had to look away, his breathing coming out shallow and raspy.

"You … you can cause ultimate chaos with the noise of war. You can bring the world to its knees by causing excruciating, unbearable noise that sparks global rage and hate. And with the shield's power, you'd be … unbeatable," Everett whispered, trying to prove to Homados that he was knowledgeable, that he approved of his plan and might be worth keeping around.

Everett had no doubt that as soon as he was no use to a power-hungry god like Homados, he would be disposed of swiftly.

"Tell me who has the Eye of Horus, Croft," Homados demanded in a low, gravelly voice that no one could ever deny. "They must hand it over willingly for its power to work."

Everett grimaced. "Ah. You might have some trouble there."

The ground shook as Homados strode over to Everett, who squealed in terror as Homados grabbed him and pinned him against the wall.

"*What did you say?*" Homados spat, reducing Everett to a quivering wreck.

"I … I only mean that you'll have to go a different way about it!" Everett croaked, his eyes wide with panic. "I am on your side, oh powerful Homados! I am at your mercy! But this person who has the Eye of Horus, they … they don't share our vision for the world."

Homados narrowed his eyes, his grasp on Everett tightening.

"But I have … an idea!" Everett said through wheezes. "I can help you. If you allow me to work with you, I can persuade her to hand over the Eye of Horus willingly."

"Why should I trust you, Croft?" Homados questioned.

"Because, more than anything, I would like to be a part of her downfall," Everett managed to say through gritted teeth. "Please. Let me help you."

After a moment of consideration, Homados let him go.

Everett gasped for air, one hand pressed against his chest as his heart thudded uncontrollably beneath it. The god kept his eyes fixed on Everett, testing him.

"I promise you, Homados," Everett said quietly but surely. "I will find a way to persuade her to give you the Eye of Horus. And then the shield, along with the world, will be yours."

His dark eyes flashing with hunger, Homados began to cackle until it grew into a laugh so frenzied and violent that, despite his new alliance, Everett Croft trembled with fear as all the windows of his tower began to shake, and somewhere across the city a girl sat up in bed suddenly filled with unexplained dread.

CHAPTER ONE

With a dramatic sigh, I bury my head in my hands and groan in frustration at my desk.

"Why is this so difficult?" I ask myself out loud. "What is *wrong* with me?"

Since I got home from school earlier this afternoon, I'm supposed to have been writing a chapter of my book, but I've been sitting here with my iPad for half an hour, and so far I have written a total of *zero* words.

It's official: I have writer's block. That wouldn't be such a big deal if I'd written something good the day before, or the day before that, but it's been a while since I've written anything at all, no matter how many times I've sat at this desk ready to start.

"This is hopeless," I say quietly, lowering my hands

to my lap, my shoulders slumping forward in defeat. "What am I doing? Why am I even *trying*?"

I hear my guide dog Maisie rise from her bed and come plodding over to me in response to my question, sitting down at my side and resting her head on my knee. I can't help but smile, reaching to stroke the soft fur of her head. She exhales in contentment and then licks my hand gently.

"Thanks, Maisie," I say, swallowing the lump in my throat. "It's nice to know that you believe in me. I just… I need a wave of inspiration, I guess."

She snorts excitedly, lifting her head in hope, her tail wagging so much I can hear it thudding against the leg of my desk.

"Oh, you think *another* walk is a good idea, do you?" I chuckle, giving her chin a scratch. "Nice try, but I'm done walking for the day. Next suggestion please."

Giving a small huff in disagreement, she leaves my side for a moment before returning, dropping a soft cuddly toy in my lap.

"Again, thank you for the kind offer, but I don't think playing with you and your toy unicorn will help me write this book, either."

I hold the unicorn out for her, and she happily

takes it from my grasp. I hear her throw the toy up in the air for herself before pouncing on it, carrying it in her jaws as she circles the floor of my bedroom triumphantly. Meanwhile, I sit back in my chair and twirl the pendant hanging round my neck with my fingers, wishing things were as simple as a cuddly unicorn sweeping all your problems away.

I know it sounds dramatic, but right from the moment I woke up this morning, I could sense it was going to be a bad day. I sat bolt upright, fully awake and with something heavy weighing on my heart. I don't know how to explain it, but something felt off. It was such a strong feeling that I even mentioned it to my older sister Poppy at breakfast, but she just huffily replied, "Oh, great, you have to say that today when I have the first round of my tennis tournament. Way to make me feel confident, Ella!"

And then she stomped out of the room.

I guess it was a bit of a negative start to the day. I'd forgotten she had that tennis match this afternoon, which goes to show how weird I was feeling because Poppy hasn't shut up about the tournament all week.

"This tournament is a *big* deal," she emphasized to me, Mum and Dad over dinner a few days ago. "All of the local schools are taking part, so if I win then I'm practically guaranteed to make captain of the tennis team next year. Kayleigh is really good, so she's my main competition, but it's hardly fair because I'm on the football and rounders teams, too, so I don't have as much time to practise as she does. Argh, I'm so *nervous!*"

"You'll do brilliantly, Poppy, I know it," Mum assured her in that calm but firm manner that doctors have a knack of pulling off. "With your drive and focus, you'll certainly be a force to be reckoned with."

We all agreed with her there. Poppy is so determined to win – she's spent every spare moment practising. I'm pleased she's found her passion for sport again – she got so wrapped up in trying to be popular for a while, and gain as many social media followers as possible, that she forgot what she loved doing – but the truth is, I miss her.

It feels like it's been a while since we spent time together properly. I get that she feels like she's playing catch-up, and she wants to impress the coaches by proving to them that she's serious about being on the sports teams again, but that means she's spending every afternoon after school and most of the weekends either playing in matches or practising for them. I'm so proud of her, I am, but I miss hanging out with her.

I can't tell her that, though. I have to be supportive.

Maybe that feeling is exaggerated anyway because my best friend Finn is so busy at the moment, too. Normally we spend a lot of time together, but since he got on this work experience programme at London Zoo I've hardly spoken to him outside of school. As well as being a total book and mythology nerd, Finn loves animals, and when he got the chance to shadow Meg – one of the keepers at the zoo – he didn't hesitate to take it. I love hearing his animal stories and he never fails to make me laugh; I'm happy for him, and for Poppy too, but it's hard not to feel left behind sometimes. And if I'm honest, I don't understand how they can carry on like everything is normal.

For them, it seems as though the Day of Darkness never happened.

Maybe I'm being unfair. It's probably a good thing that they're focusing on what's ahead rather than dwelling on something that happened in the past. But it's different for me. I can't move on as easily. Maybe it's because I don't share the same sense of relief that the world went back to being just as it was before. Maybe I wanted things to change.

I *do* want things to change.

When Lugh took the light and the world was plunged into darkness, I never expected to be the one who would have to save the day. I never thought I would meet Ailynn, the owner of the Mythos Library, who would tell me that the key to defeating Lugh lay with seven stones that were created by ancient druids and could channel the magic of the rainbow. Maisie and I never expected to lead Poppy and Finn on a quest around London to collect those stones, and I *definitely* never thought we'd find a way to change Lugh's mind about people so he'd return the light to the world without us having to defeat him at all. But all of that happened. I have the Eye of Horus to prove it, the pendant that Lugh gave to me as a gift.

We brought light back to every country, every nation, every person on the planet. We *saved the world*. And then … everything went back to how it was.

I thought that the Day of Darkness would trigger more change. The world would become more accessible and more understanding. Things would be *better*. Everyone knew now what it was like, for everything to turn to darkness. Everyone had experienced the fear and the challenges that come with that, just like I did when I lost my sight because of a degenerative eye disease. I believed that when the darkness lifted, people would wake up to the small but significant changes that could be made to make my world better.

They didn't.

I still overhear people muttering complaints under their breath about my guide dog in restaurants; public transport is still daunting for me to use; shops are still tricky to navigate independently. How is it possible that I saved the world and yet I still feel an inconvenience to it?

Even though Poppy, Finn and I decided to keep our adventures secret, I wanted to write a book inspired by our adventures. I've always wanted to write and now I had my story. It makes perfect sense to devote myself to my new writing project, especially as Poppy and Finn are so busy with their passions and hobbies. But it's not going well. The inspiration is falling flat.

I drop my hand from the Eye of Horus pendant, and I'm about to push myself up off the chair to go downstairs and wallow on the sofa when I hear a knock on the door to my room. It swings open before I can answer, bumping against the wall.

"Oh my god, Ella, you won't believe what happened today," Poppy announces as she flounces in and I hear her slump down on my bed.

"Hey! What are you doing home? I thought you had the first round of your tennis tournament."

"Yeah, we were supposed to, but it's been cancelled!"

"What? How come?"

"The weather! Duh! It's pouring. Haven't you noticed?" She stomps loudly from my bed over to the window. "It's, like, a full-on storm out there. It's meant to be the summer. I don't understand, it was sunny this morning. Dad told me this wasn't even forecasted."

Now that I really listen, I can hear the rain hammering down hard outside. I must have been so wrapped up in my own thoughts, I hadn't noticed before.

"Couldn't they have moved it to indoor courts somewhere?" I reason.

"Not with such late notice. Now we have to play next week instead."

"Oh! So, it hasn't been cancelled, it's just been postponed."

"Ella, that is not the point," she snaps. "I was ready

to play today, now I'll have to get my head all riled up again for the match on Tuesday. And I'm meant to have football practice on Tuesday lunchtime. I'll have to miss it now."

"Why? Won't the tournament be after school?"

"*Yes*," she says, exasperated, "but I can't risk getting injured, can I? What if I went over on my ankle or something during a tackle right before the first round of the tennis tournament? I'll have to miss out on football practice that day which doesn't look good when I'm trying to prove I'm captain material. Argh! This is so *unfair*! Honestly, Ella, you were right about all those bad omens, or whatever you were saying about today, because the *worst* has happened, and I feel like this keeps happening to me lately…"

As she rants on, I try my best to focus on listening and sympathizing with her rather than give in to the temptation to shout out loud all the negative thoughts that cloud my brain as she speaks: *How did we go from saving the world from eternal darkness to you caring so much about* this? *Don't you realize how trivial these problems sound? Don't you ever think about what happened? Why does no one else care?*

I think I might be having a bad day. Those questions seem louder than ever today.

"And to top things off, I bought a doughnut on the way home and then a pigeon flew right at me, like right at my *face*, and I screamed and dropped it." She pauses to take a deep breath. "You know what, Ella? The world hates me today."

"I'm sorry you feel like that."

She exhales dramatically. "Yeah, well, things have got to get better otherwise I'm going to lose it."

I hesitate, before tentatively saying, "Hey, can I ask you something? Do you ever ... think about the Day of Darkness?"

Poppy snorts. "What kind of question is that? Of course I do. It was a big deal."

"Yeah, exactly," I say, her response giving me confidence to carry on. "It *was* a big deal. Sometimes I find it hard to concentrate on everyday things because I'm distracted by everything that happened and how ... how I thought more changes would come about because of it all."

"What do you mean?"

"I find it hard that people don't seem to care about what—"

"It's not that people don't care, Ella," she cuts in. "But you can't dwell on the past. You have to look to the future, right? Everything's OK now."

"But that's my point. Everything's not—"

"Wait, sorry, Ella, someone is calling me. Oh, it's Kayleigh. I have to get this." She clears her throat and answers her phone. "Hi, Kayleigh! Yeah, I know, can you believe it? I *know*! What did Coach say to you? Uh-huh. Yeah, I thought that."

Poppy marches out of my room, striding across the landing before going into her bedroom and slamming the door behind her, leaving me alone once again with a sinking heart and a blank page.

CHAPTER TWO

"Are you OK?" Finn asks me the next day at lunchtime in the school canteen.

"I'm fine," I say, shifting in my seat. "Why?"

"You've barely touched your food. You've been quiet today. Are you upset about what Mrs McCabe said this morning?"

I shake my head. In our maths lesson earlier, we got our marked homework back and I'd got a low grade which prompted Mrs McCabe to comment on my "distinct lack of effort". Although maths has never been my strong point, I don't usually do *this* badly. I've been distracted. I forgot about the maths assignment until the night before and had to do a rush job on it, so I wasn't surprised about the grade.

"You know what Mrs McCabe is like," Finn says,

apparently convinced that my insignificant maths homework is the cause of what's troubling me. "She has such high expectations. In a way, it's a good thing. She expects better from you. She doesn't expect *anything* from me."

I can't help but break into a smile.

"That's not true," I say.

"It is. I swear she's out to get me. Did I tell you she got cross at me last week for running down the corridor? Then, when I was late to her lesson that *same day*, she asked me why I hadn't rushed to be there! She doesn't like me, and you know why?"

"Because you make it obvious that you'd much rather be in English class or in the library reading books, or literally *anywhere else* but her maths class?" I say, amused.

"OK, fine, maybe that's part of the reason why –" he pauses as I shake my head at him, chuckling "– but the main reason is because of sloths."

"Sloths?"

"Yes, *sloths*," he tells me conspiratorially. "When I stepped into the staffroom for all of two seconds looking for Mr Wilson to ask him a question about this book he'd recommended to me, she shooed me out and then told me off for looking so scruffy, ordering me to sort out my collar and tuck my shirt in. She said I looked like a lazy sloth."

"And?"

"So I did what anyone would do. I told her that she was wrong. Sloths are not lazy at all! They have evolved to move slowly as a *survival* strategy."

I try to suppress a smirk. "Really."

"Yeah, Meg told me all about it when I helped her with the sloths at the zoo. Basically, they have to move slowly in the trees due to their poor eyesight and the fact that they have an extremely slow rate of digestion due to their four-chambered stomach – they are constantly saving energy. And why do they need to outrun predators when they can hide from them? They chill in the trees, eating the leaves which are their main source of diet, relying on the camouflage they have up there and going completely unnoticed by predators like jaguars and eagles. You know what that is? *Genius* survival tactics."

"So you're saying that sloths do everything in slow motion not because they're lazy but because they're smart," I check.

"Exactly," he tells me matter-of-factly. "It's evolution! They have no need to rush anything so they don't. It's more beneficial for them in so many ways to be slow. Why do people think sloths have lasted this long? If you think sloths are lazy then you're an idiot."

I hesitate. "Finn?"

"Yes?"

"Did you say *all* of that to Mrs McCabe when she compared you to a lazy sloth?"

"Yeah! It's interesting, useful knowledge."

"Even the last part? About how you're … an *idiot* if you think sloths are lazy? Right after she'd said that sloths are lazy?"

There's a beat of silence.

"Oh. Yes, I did," he admits. "Now you say it like that, I can see why she got so cross and gave me detention."

I start giggling, which causes Finn to break into an infectious chuckle, making me laugh even harder. I feel my mood lift as I sit opposite my best friend, clutching my stomach and wheezing with laughter.

"I can't believe you called Mrs McCabe an idiot!"

"I can't believe I called Mrs McCabe an idiot without even realizing!" he adds, and we both burst out laughing again.

I pick up my fork, suddenly feeling hungry as my giggles subside. "Finn, can you use the clock method

25

to tell me where everything is on my plate? I've forgotten."

"Sure," he says cheerfully. "OK, so at twelve o'clock you have the veggie lasagne, at three o'clock you have the peas, at six o'clock there's the carrots, and at nine o'clock some salad. Do you want some ketchup for the lasagne?"

I grin wider. "You know me so well."

"There's none on the table, I'll go get you some, hang on."

"Thank you."

I hear the legs of his chair scrape back from the table as he gets up and I make a start on my vegetables while I wait for him to return with the ketchup bottle. I'm still smiling about his misstep with Mrs McCabe, the strictest and grumpiest teacher in the school, when I hear a muttered comment from the table behind me that attracts my attention.

"I just don't understand why dogs would be allowed in here."

My fork pauses midway to my mouth. I don't know the voice, it's a girl, maybe someone in a year or two above us because she doesn't sound familiar. My heart begins to thud loudly, my stomach twisting with nerves. Maybe I misheard. Maybe she wasn't talking about my guide dog lying down perfectly at my feet. I'm sure that she wasn't—

"Having a dog in this canteen, especially a hairy dog like that, is unhygienic," she continues in a low hushed voice. "I like dogs but not around my food, you know?"

There's a ripple of whispered agreements from her friends.

I drop my fork to my tray and spin in my seat to face them.

"Maisie is a guide dog," I snap loudly, prompting the tables surrounding ours to fall into a hush as everyone listens in. "I have the right to be accompanied by her wherever I go, including this canteen and any restaurants open to anyone else. She is a working dog, not a pet, don't you understand that?"

Silence roars through the canteen.

"Uh … I, sorry," the girl replies meekly, "I didn't mean—"

"Maisie isn't bothering you, she's not stealing your food or begging for it, she's not jumping up on any of the chairs or tables, she's sitting here at my feet perfectly still, just as she's trained to do, so I don't know why you needed to say any of those things about her."

I'm greeted with more silence. My jaw tenses as I continue to wait for her reply.

Eventually someone standing over me clears their throat and I realize that Finn has made his way back and is standing by my side.

"Hey," he says gently, "are you all right?"

"Fine," I mumble, standing up, my hand gripping Maisie's harness tightly as she gets to her feet. "I'm not hungry any more."

My cheeks flushing with heat, I give Maisie her instruction: "Forward."

As we walk out of the canteen, I know I should keep my head held high in the knowledge that I stood up for what was right. Instead I feel deflated, humiliated and exhausted. The world turned dark and that still wasn't enough for me to be seen as equal.

What will it take?

I realize too late that in the heat of the moment I've left my tray for Finn to clear up, which isn't very thoughtful of me, but I can't go back now. When I hear footsteps catching up with mine as I walk down the empty corridor from the canteen, I assume it's Finn and prepare to thank him for sorting the trays so speedily, but I soon realize it's not him.

"Hey, Ella," someone calls out, and it's a boy's voice I don't recognize.

I bring Maisie to a stop, already feeling defensive, prepared to argue my case.

"Hi," he says as he moves to stand in front of me. "You're Ella Jones, right? I'm River. I'm sorry about what happened just now, I—"

"OK, I'm sorry if I upset your friend, I shouldn't have spoken to her like that in front of everyone," I say impatiently, trying to navigate my feelings of anger and guilt, "but she embarrassed me, too. It's important for her to understand why service dogs like Maisie have the legal right to be in that canteen and if she's so unhappy about it, then maybe she should eat somewhere else."

"I agree."

I pause, stunned. "You … you do?"

"Yeah, I do," he confirms. "I'm not one of her friends. Sorry, I should have explained – I'm new here at this school. I started today and I'm in your class."

"Oh. *Oh!*" I nod, blushing all over again as I realize that in our form room this morning during registration the teacher introduced a new kid called River. "Sorry, I thought you were her friend coming to tell me off."

"No, I was in the canteen and heard what happened and I wanted to make sure you're OK. I thought you handled that situation well."

I hang my head. "No, I didn't. I should be more patient. Not everyone will understand how it is."

"Maybe, but you'd think they would after the Day of Darkness."

I snap my head up. "*Right?* That's what I think!"

"Yeah, it baffles me." He sighs heavily. "Anyway, I wanted to properly introduce myself to you. I'm River, I have blond hair, blue eyes and I'm about a foot taller than you – all my family are tall. Are you a handshaker?"

"Sure." I hold out my hand and he takes it. "Nice to meet you, River."

"Nice to meet *you*, Ella."

"And this is Maisie," I tell him.

"I won't pet her as she's got her harness on and I know she's working, but it's nice to meet you both. Where were you heading?"

"I'm not sure," I admit with a shrug. "I just wanted to get out of there."

"Well, we've still got twenty minutes of lunchbreak left. It's been cloudy all morning but the sun has come out. Do you want to go sit outside and you can fill me in on everything about the school?"

"Yeah, I do," I say, breaking into a wide grin. "Maisie, forward."

"Great, I need all the help I can get," he sighs, walking along next to me as we make our way down the corridor towards the exit. "It's only my first day and I already got in trouble with a teacher because my shirt was untucked."

"Was it Mrs McCabe?"

"That's the one! How did you know it was her?"

"Lucky guess," I say, as he pulls the door open for me and we stroll out into the sunshine.

CHAPTER THREE

"Are you *serious*?" River cries, his locker door squeaking as he closes it. "You've never played a video game?"

"I think I tried playing a game at a friend's house a few years ago, but I can't remember," I admit, chuckling at his astounded reaction. "I definitely haven't played one recently. I haven't really thought to."

"OK, well that's going to change," he states as though there's no other option. "There are some brilliant accessible games, one of my favourites – which is about these characters in a post-apocalyptic world – has detailed audio cues. It's so fun, you have to try it." He hesitates. "Maybe you and Finn could come round to my house one day after school and we could play it on my PlayStation if you like?"

"That sounds great!" I say brightly, before adding, "If Finn *ever* gets a free afternoon from the zoo. Thanks, River."

"No problem," he says, and I can hear the excitement in his voice.

Ever since River introduced himself last week, we've become friends quickly. He seemed so confident when he approached me that day after the canteen incident, but I've realized that he's not like that with everyone. He's shy and introverted, especially in class where he barely says a word. But when we spend time together during breaks, he comes right out of his shell, forgets about everyone around him, and, depending on the topic, can be chatty.

I've noticed he doesn't like talking about himself much, but it's obvious we're into similar things, like fantasy and sci-fi books and TV. He loves dogs too, so he's comfortable with Maisie. We went to the park after school earlier this week so she could have a good run and River loved playing with her once I took her harness off.

"I keep seeing you with that new kid at school, the tall one," Poppy observed during dinner yesterday when Mum was on shift at the hospital and Dad had taken a work call in his office.

"River. He's great," I told her enthusiastically. "Finn has promised to come here on Saturday to watch *Doctor Who* with me and I might ask River if he wants to come too as I know he's a big fan, so you can meet him then!"

"Ah. He's a *Doctor Who* fan. Makes sense."

"What do you mean? What makes sense?" I asked, confused.

"Why you'd get on well so quickly. The three of you all like the same nerdy stuff," she said, chuckling. "No offence."

"None taken," I said, sitting up straighter. "And don't pretend like you don't like 'nerdy stuff', too. Remember the Christmas Special on TV last year when you got all stroppy about having to watch it and then you were asking a million questions about all the characters because you were so invested?"

"I have no idea what you're talking about," she said breezily.

Smiling, I reached for my water and took a sip while she waited for Dad to come back in, launching into a conversation about his latest publicity project. Poppy and I both know that if she ends up being free on Saturday, she'll make a big fuss about not watching "Doctor Dork", as she calls it, but then will slip in the room to sneakily get involved.

I hope she does.

When I mentioned the *Doctor Who* plans to River this morning, he was keen, so hopefully Finn hasn't forgotten either. Our conversation somehow moved on to video games and I quickly found out that River is big on gaming. I like the idea of going to River's house some time, since I don't know much about his family. I've asked him a few questions about them and the school he went to before this one, but his answers have been vague and short.

"It would be cool to hear what you think of the stories in some of the PS games," he tells me now, as we leave the lockers to head to the auditorium for morning assembly. "As a writer yourself you can let me know if you think the plots are any good. Sometimes I think they're just as good as movies. It's an art form."

"I'm not a writer, River," I laugh.

"You told me you're writing a book."

"Yeah, which is currently about two pages long," I scoff. "I can't seem to write more."

"That's all part of the process," he insists, as Maisie slows when we join the back of the crowd of students filing into the auditorium in front of us. "I met a fantasy author once and he said that it took him *years* to write his first book and now all his books are movies! He also told me that his first drafts are completely different to the final book that goes to print. So, there you go. Writer's block and going back and forth on a plot is all part of it."

"Wow! How did you meet him?" I ask, intrigued.

"Oh, at one of my parents' parties," he says dismissively.

"Sounds glamorous."

He hesitates. "Not really."

I get the feeling that he doesn't want to expand on it any further, so I don't ask him any more questions even though I want to. I wonder who his parents are and what they do to be able to throw parties attended by famous authors.

When we get to our seats, I say "Under" to Maisie so she knows to settle under my legs, and we wait for assembly to start. Finn comes to find us a few minutes later, sounding flustered as he takes the seat on the other side of River.

"How come you're late?" I whisper now that a hush is descending across the room.

"The lioness at the zoo is pregnant and I got up

super early this morning to go see if today was the big day," he answers excitedly. "Meg told me off for risking being late to school and she's promised to message me if anything happens. Imagine, Ella – *lion cubs*! How cool is that?"

I manage a quick nod, a lump building in my throat at the flashback I'm experiencing of our encounter in the lion enclosure on the Day of Darkness.

One of the rainbow stones was hidden there and if I think too long on it, I feel just as scared as I was that day as we quietly made our way through the zoo knowing the animals were roaming freely, listening out for poisonous snakes and hungry tigers. I can still smell the overwhelming stench of poo that filled my nostrils because the zoo had been quickly abandoned by its terrified keepers. I remember feeling too frightened to breathe and how my blood turned to ice when we heard the low, rumbling growl of an approaching lion.

A shiver rolls down my spine and I'm genuinely relieved when our head teacher steps on to the stage and begins to read out the boring school notices. She's in the middle of an announcement about how to sign up to volunteer for the new litter-picking initiative when I realize the Eye of Horus is growing warm at my neck. Placing my fingers on the pendant, I feel how unusually hot to touch it is. I shift in my seat as I'm filled with a weird sense of unease.

"Are you OK, Ella?" River whispers.

"Yeah, fine," I say.

I don't tell him the truth, but for some reason I have a weird sense that something bad is about to happen. And that's when I hear something strange: a low background noise of traffic. At first, it's not too loud, just a heightened din of the roads nearby: cars beeping in annoyance, the squeaking and hissing sound of bus doors opening and closing, music blaring from radios. It's unusual because I've never been able to hear that from inside the school before. It's ... getting louder. And becoming distracting.

"What is that?" River whispers, as I feel him shift uncomfortably next to me.

"Maybe something's happened on the road," I reply, frowning as it intensifies.

Even the head teacher is faltering now, her sentence trailing off as she lets out an exasperated "*Really!*", frustrated at the disturbance.

The sound of sirens pierces through the air and a mounting sense of confusion fills the auditorium as the noise continues to grow.

"What is going on?" Finn asks anxiously as the students erupt into complaints.

"Why does it feel like we're in the middle of traffic on a motorway?" River says through gritted teeth, his arm brushing against mine as he lifts his hand to cover his ear. "Argh! Make it stop! It feels like the traffic is in my head now!"

"This is horrible!" Finn whimpers. "The scraping and screeching! I hate that sound! Stop it!"

My breathing starts coming out shaky and uneven as panic grips the room. The noise is almost unbearable now and I yelp as it overwhelms every other sense, causing an instant headache. People are yelling now, shouting angrily at their companions about why it's happening, begging anyone to bring it to a stop and crying out in frustration as the noise builds and builds until it's impossible to do or think of anything else.

As I begin to lose myself in the horror of this feeling, I feel Maisie nudge urgently at my leg. My hand falls to the top of her head and drifts down her back, and I can feel that she's breathing normally. She's calm and controlled, unaffected and right here with me.

A memory from a couple of years ago battles its way to the forefront of my mind:

I'm sitting at the kitchen table with Gavin, the mobility instructor who helped me navigate my new world when I first lost my sight and had to re-learn everyday tasks again. I'm having a bad day. I've tried to pour a glass of water and it's gone everywhere. On some days, Poppy and I laugh about these things. Other days, we cry.

Today, I'm crying.

The reality that I won't be able to do simple things on my own, like pour a glass of water without it feeling like a big, daunting task engulfs me. Walking out the door by myself will be difficult. How am I supposed to get excited about my future when making a cup of tea will be a challenge? I'm exhausted from the amount of focus and energy it takes to learn everything again. I'm angry that this has happened to me. I feel alone, no matter how much love and support my family gives. It feels like I'm … stranded.

I don't say all this to Gavin. Instead I say, "It's too much."

"Yes, it's a lot," he replies simply. "You'll get there, one step at a time."

I sniff, shaking my head. "It doesn't feel that way."

He takes a moment and then says, "I know it's overwhelming. I know it feels like you're crumbling,

but this – all of it – will show you what you're made of."

In the midst of the unbearable noise roaring through the auditorium, Maisie nudges my leg again. Her soothing presence brings me back. I won't let what's happening right now make me crumble. I will accept it and find my way through it. Instead of focusing on the sense of panic that this overwhelming noise threatens, I try to focus on something simple: my breathing. Deep breath in, long exhale out. Feel the cool air as it fills my lungs, breathe out the warm air. With one hand on Maisie's head, her thick, soft fur warm against my leg, I gradually begin to steady my breathing.

The Eye of Horus pendant remains warm against my skin. I realize it's helping to calm me. And now that I've collected myself, I'm able to listen properly. I'm not shying away from the noise. There, among the traffic sounds reverberating in my ears, is something else, something out of place and distant. It takes a moment to work out what it reminds me of, then I realize it's like a battle scene in a movie: swords clashing, shields blocking, arrows zipping.

Strange.

Suddenly the noise stops. The panic begins to lift. I can hear everyone gasping for breath as they recover. The whole school is in a state of shock.

"What was *that*?" Finn asks through wheezes, his voice wobbling.

"I have no idea," I reply, reaching to touch my pendant as its warmth fades. "But I hope it doesn't happen again."

CHAPTER FOUR

The auditorium erupts into panicked and worried conversation as everyone tries to understand what just happened. We begin to realize that whatever that noise was, it didn't just happen here – phones throughout the auditorium vibrate and beep as family and friends describe their own experience and check in on each other. Our head teacher tries to regain control of the room, but she sounds as thrown as anyone, and in the end, she tells us to please return to our form rooms.

"That was the weirdest thing I've ever felt," Finn says in shock, as we follow the other students leaving the room. "I couldn't shut out the noise even though I covered my ears!"

"It made my brain hurt," River says wearily.

"It made my whole body hurt," Finn adds.

Suddenly, I hear Poppy's voice calling my name as she makes her way through the crowd to link her arm with mine as Maisie leads the way to my form room.

"Ella, are you OK?" Poppy asks anxiously. "That was horrible!"

"I'm fine," I assure her, my heart swelling at how, no matter how much we bicker or how cool she plays it at school, it will always be instinctive to Poppy to play the part of protective older sister. "Are you all right?"

"I think so. I thought my brain might explode from the sound, though. It was like a mixture of loud sirens, nails scratching on a chalkboard and metal scraping – *ugh*." She groans, squeezing my arm. "Even thinking about it gives me a headache. Did anyone else feel … *angry*, too?"

Finn gasps behind us. "Yes! I thought that was just me."

"No, I felt that, too," River chips in. "Like boiling-hot rage bubbling through me."

"And when I let that rage out, it helped," Finn admits quietly. "I feel so guilty for shouting, but I couldn't help it."

"Exactly. I yelled at Kayleigh who was next to me,

but it wasn't her fault, and she was shrieking back at me," Poppy says, before she exhales the air from her cheeks. "Weird."

I stay quiet, deep in thought. Although I experienced the same panic and confusion, I don't remember feeling uncontrollable anger. My free hand flies up to the Eye of Horus. It definitely connected with me somehow. I think back on what Lugh said when he gifted it to me: "*The symbol of an eye, it represents healing and protection, a beacon of light and hope... As long as you're wearing this, Ella, it will protect you and those you love from any danger wielded by the gods... Human folly you'll have to fend off by yourself.*"

During that unbearable noise, the Eye of Horus came to life. It grew hot, as though something inside of it was glowing. I think it was doing its job: protecting me.

Which means that what just happened wasn't the work of a human.

It was the work of a god.

"Ella, are you sure you're OK?" Poppy asks, jolting me from my thoughts. "You look like you're in shock. I'm sure we can ask to go home for the rest of the day if you need."

"No, I'm fine, I promise," I tell her, plastering on a smile.

I don't want to mention my suspicions and give them any unnecessary worry. It could have been coincidental that my pendant grew warm at the same time. I hope that it was.

"Ella was the only person who *was* fine!" A boy says, overhearing our conversation and joining in as Maisie brings me to a stop outside my form room. "I saw you, Ella, I was in the row behind you. Everyone else was in pain or whatever and you looked like you couldn't hear a thing! You were so still!"

"I did hear it," I tell him, heat flushing my face as I guiltily think about the pendant. "I … I just … I tried to focus on listening through the chaos of the noise."

"That makes sense," he says excitedly, "because you're used to hearing so well since going blind, right? You have, like, super-hearing now, so I figured all that loud noise was probably almost normal for you."

I hear Poppy sigh irritably beside me.

"Uh, no, I don't have super-hearing," I inform him, ready to reel out my usual explanation to this familiar misunderstanding. "Just because I'm blind doesn't mean my other senses are heightened or anything like that. I had to learn to listen to what was important – sounds that I might not have noticed before I lost my sight but are now key to my mobility."

"Wait, so … it's not like … Daredevil?" he checks.

"Daredevil was blinded by a radioactive substance that heightens his senses beyond human ability," Finn explains to him. "*That's* why he has supersonic hearing."

"Oh. OK." He sounds disappointed.

I hear the squeak of his shoes as he turns and continues down the corridor, while Poppy moves to stand in front of me.

"Is that true?" she asks.

"That I'm not Daredevil? I'm afraid so."

"I meant is it true you managed to stay calm during whatever that noise was?" she says, amused at my joke. I can practically hear her rolling her eyes – it's not the first time someone has assumed that as soon as I went blind, my hearing gained superpowers.

"Sort of. At first I didn't. I focused on what Gavin taught me," I explain away, playing it down.

She sighs. "I had better get to my class. I'll come find you later."

We wave her off and then I instruct Maisie to go

into the classroom and find my desk. Our teacher asks us all to try to stay calm while we wait for some answers, recommending that we focus on homework for now. But there's no chance anyone can think or talk about anything else. It's a strange atmosphere for the rest of the day as the teachers try to make things run as normal, but everyone feels on edge – students and teachers.

And all the while I try to convince myself that it was a freak one-off incident that will have a perfectly reasonable explanation, when deep in my heart I think I know that it doesn't. If the Day of Darkness taught me anything, it's that sometimes the explanation isn't reasonable at all. Sometimes, it's beyond anything you can imagine.

Sometimes it's gods playing games.

That evening, it happens again.

I'm sitting on my duvet with Mum going through my make-up bag and applying Braille to all my new items while Maisie has curled up in her bed with her unicorn. Mum bought me some amazing new products recently – I think she's picked up on me being a little down the last week or so and wanted to cheer me up – but all the packaging feels the same, so

I can't work out which tube is concealer and which is primer, or tell the lip gloss from the mascara.

"OK, so this is the liquid blush," Mum says, handing it over so I can carefully apply the Braille label I'd prepared on to the tube. "And up next is the concealer. I might ask if I can borrow this from you some time. It looks nice."

"You can borrow it anytime," I say, smiling at her. "At least you *ask*, unlike Poppy."

"I think you give as good as you get. Didn't you borrow her lip gloss without asking?"

"Only because she always uses mine!"

"And you helped yourself to one of her perfumes when she was out."

"I spritzed some on my wrist to try it," I huff defensively. "She made that into a *much* bigger deal than it was. What about my jewellery that she wears? Or all my hair products that she uses in the bathroom? She goes on at me for even *thinking* about using some of her expensive shampoo then she uses all my conditioning treatments."

Mum chuckles. "You're lucky. Having a sister means you can share everything."

"Sharing is one word for it. In her case, I'd call it stealing."

From her corner, Maisie lets out a grumble in solidarity.

"I hope Poppy's training session is going OK," Mum says. "After what happened this morning, I thought she might want to come home sooner but she refused." She sighs. "I read that they think it might have been some kind of coordinated technological blip."

I don't say anything. Mum must read my silent reaction as fear, because she quickly lifts her tone when she speaks, sounding bizarrely bright and chirpy as though there's absolutely nothing in the whole wide world to worry about. I think she's trying to convince herself as much as me.

"Hey, I have an idea!" she exclaims. "How about we treat ourselves to hot chocolate?"

I balk at the suggestion. "It's a warm evening."

"So? You think hot chocolate is only allowed in winter months? Not on my watch!"

I hear her jump to her feet and stride out the room determinedly, before she heads downstairs and knocks on Dad's office door to offer him a mug, too.

"Hot chocolate?" I hear him say, flabbergasted. "It's summer!"

"Why do people think hot chocolate is only

allowed in winter?" Mum cries, the exasperation in her voice making me giggle.

"You know what? You're right," Dad squeaks hurriedly. "We should have it all year round, whenever we feel like it. And I feel like some now. So, yes please to hot chocolate."

"Correct answer," Mum declares triumphantly.

While she busies herself downstairs in the kitchen, I listen to a message River has sent about a book, using my phone's VoiceOver to read it aloud. I'm about to dictate a reply when my pendant grows warm and I hear the noise. It's faint at first but terrifyingly familiar: a background din of clashing and scraping. My breath catching in my throat, I lower my phone. Having seen my reaction, Maisie snorts and gets up to come over to the bed. I reach for her, my hand trembling as I place it on her head.

Suddenly, it's as though someone turns up the volume.

The noise becomes so loud, I wince at the roar in my ears, my free hand flying to press against my forehead as it begins to ache. There's something different about the noise this time. Among all the fighting and screaming and scraping, I can hear the faint sound of something else in the distance. I think it's a man *laughing*. Laughing at the suffering.

The thought fills me with dread.

Deep breaths, Ella, deep breaths, I tell myself. *You've been here. You've made your way through this before, and you can do it again.*

As I inhale deeply through my nose, Maisie lifts her snout to lick my hand. She's letting me know she's here, like always. I'm not alone. The Eye of Horus grows warmer and warmer. Calm ripples through me and the noise doesn't overwhelm me any more. It's still there, but I can distance myself from it. I can drown it out with positive thoughts and fierce focus. Beyond the noise, I hear the sound of something breaking downstairs in the kitchen: a mug dropping and smashing across the tiles. I can hear my parents crying out, shouting for it to stop. My heart beats faster but not in fear or panic – it quickens in determination.

Getting off the bed, I make my way out on to the landing, finding the banister and walking downstairs with Maisie right at my feet, refusing to leave my side. I reach Dad's office first and hear him yelling from low on the ground. He must be kneeling or crouching, finding the noise so excruciating he's slid from his chair to the floor.

"Dad! Dad, it's OK, it's going to be OK," I say, focusing on finding his voice through the din.

"Make it stop!" he shouts, and I hear him thump his fist repeatedly on the carpet.

"Dad, I'm here," I say, kneeling down in front of him and reaching out.

As soon as I place my hands on his arm, he inhales sharply. I feel the tension in his body ease.

"Ella, it's you," he says breathlessly, the anger in his voice vanishing. "Are you OK? What is this?"

"I don't know. Can you still hear it, too?"

"Yes," he answers, taking my hands in his. "But it doesn't hurt any more now you're here. You've made it … fade."

Then the noise lifts altogether. Silence descends over the house.

After checking I'm all right, Dad gets up to rush into the kitchen to check on Mum. He calls out that she's fine – she dropped a mug of hot chocolate, that's all. Both of them come rushing back to the office to pull me and Maisie into a hug before Mum quickly calls Poppy, who confirms she's OK but she's coming home now. None of us say much the rest of the evening, too shocked to talk about it.

That night, I barely sleep, Lugh's voice whirring round and round my mind on a loop:

"As long as you're wearing this, Ella, it will protect you and those you love from any danger wielded by the gods..."

CHAPTER FIVE

"I want to go to the Mythos Library and speak to Ailynn first thing tomorrow," I announce to Poppy and Finn two days later after school, stopping them at the school gates before we head home. "I think she might have some answers to the unbearable noise."

"You think that she might know something?" Poppy asks in a way that convinces me she doesn't think Ailynn will know anything at all.

"Yes," I state, already irritated at her response and on the defensive. "Don't you?"

She sighs heavily.

"Finn?" I prompt, hoping he'll fight my corner.

"Uh." He takes his time, clearly torn over what to say. "I guess it can't hurt."

Not exactly the enthusiasm I was hoping for, but it's better than nothing.

I'm baffled that they're not jumping at the chance to find out the answer to what's causing these weird stints of noise that are becoming dangerous and distracting. Yesterday, it happened during lunch break and people became so stressed and angry they started smashing plates and glasses on the floor. It was lucky Maisie and I weren't in the canteen at the time; it would have been hazardous for her to walk through afterwards. It happened again in the night, too. I sat bolt upright in my bed and clutched my pendant, which burned hot in my grasp. The noise was excruciating, and I could still hear that distant chuckle, a laugh so evil it haunted me long after the battle noise died down. As I heard my parents shouting at each other during the din, I decided I was going to see Ailynn as soon as possible. Mum and Dad hardly ever argue. And they don't fight like that. Ever.

But with every bout of noise, the anger and rage grows, and I get it. Everyone is bewildered and scared – when it happens, it brings the world to a dangerous and terrifying standstill – and no one has any answers. Well, some people *think* they do.

There are so many theories spreading online, it's impossible to list them all. One that's gaining a lot of attention is the idea that it's being caused by a big tech company channelling noise through electronic products, but the motive of that one is a bit hazy. Some people think it's because the corporation behind it is going to launch a new ear-protection product, in the same way that Everett Croft launched a light source with prior knowledge of the Day of Darkness. But so far, there've been no flashy new products released. Nothing man-made protects you from this noise. The other big theory is that it's some kind of threat from non-human bots, the first sign of a takeover by computer programs. According to Poppy, who has social media, the government has also been blamed and a theory about aliens is popular on TikTok. No one has mentioned hearing a man laughing. I can't help but feel that either I'm making it up and hearing something that's not there, or maybe … maybe that laugh is meant only for me.

"Finn, surely you agree with me that Ailynn will be able to help," I plead, taking a step towards them and lowering my voice. "I told you both about the Eye of Horus."

"You said it got warm," Poppy says carefully. "Are

you sure it did that by itself? My jewellery gets hot if I am."

"It wasn't my skin warming up the pendant, it was the pendant itself burning, like it was working magically. You remember why Lugh said that would happen," I remind them.

"That is strange," Finn comments. "And you're sure this hasn't happened before?"

"No. It only happens during the noise."

"Don't you think, before we rush to conclusions, we should consider what else the noise could be?" Poppy suggests. "Kayleigh's dad works in tech and he said it would be possible for a large corporation to pull off something like this."

I snort at the idea. "The sound doesn't come from our phones and laptops, Poppy. It's in our heads. It makes everyone angry! How could a company do that?"

"Actually, quite easily," Finn declares. "I've been reading about it and someone could have produced an anger-inducing signal of some kind that's transmitted and disguised through the noise."

"OK, but why would they do that?" I ask, bristling. "And why would my pendant work against it? Lugh said it wouldn't protect me from human action."

"He also said it would protect the people you love," Poppy mutters. "And I did not feel calm when it happened last night. I was so cross I threw my phone across the room and cracked the screen, which is a literal *nightmare*. I don't get an upgrade for, like, a year."

"I told you, when I reached Dad in his office, he was protected, too. He said that as soon as I touched him, the noise and anger faded. I think I need to be near you for it to work."

"Maybe he was comforted by his daughter being near him," she reasons.

"I don't understand this," I admit, exasperated. "You two were there with me on the Day of Darkness. You *know* Lugh exists. You know that a god's involvement could be likely!"

"We know," Finn says gently.

"But we're open to other explanations too," Poppy adds. "We don't want to rock up at the Mythos Library and demand answers."

"I wouldn't *demand* anything!"

"Come on, Ella, you know what I meant!" Poppy sounds annoyed now. "I'm not saying that you're wrong, maybe there is something to this Eye of Horus thing. Maybe it is connected. But shouldn't we do a bit of our own research first?"

"Ailynn is a fountain of all mythological knowledge, there's no need to research if we talk to her," I say through gritted teeth.

"Then why hasn't she come to you?" Poppy counters. "She knows you have the Eye of Horus. She knows what it means. If there's an obvious connection, we wouldn't need to go to her. She'd already be knocking at our door."

I open my mouth to argue back but then close it again.

She has a point.

"Why don't we wait until next week?" Finn suggests, and I can hear the strain in his voice as he tries to keep the peace between us. "Ella, if there's still no difference by Monday then we can go see Ailynn. Does that sound like a good idea?"

"I think that's fair," Poppy says, satisfied.

But I'm not. I can't explain why I'm so certain. *I just know.*

"No, I'm going to see Ailynn tomorrow morning," I say firmly. "If there's a chance that the Eye of Horus is connected to whatever is going on, then I'm not going to risk leaving it longer until it's too late to help stop it. I have to check. Will you come with me?"

Poppy heaves a sigh. "I can't. I have the second

round of my tennis tournament tomorrow. You know that."

"There's talk that schools might be closing down if this noise continues because it's becoming too disturbing!" I point out, exasperated. "There might not be any tennis tournament if it goes on."

"Which is exactly why I need to make the most of it while I still can. I can't not show up. It's important to me, Ella," she says sharply.

"Fine." I shake my head in disbelief. "What about you, Finn?"

"Ella, I want to, I do – you know I love any excuse to go to the Mythos Library," he says hurriedly. "But the lion cubs … I said I'd help Meg. It is a once in a lifetime opportunity for me." He pauses, before adding quietly, "I'm so sorry."

My heart sinks with disappointment.

I find myself nodding. "It's OK, I get it," I say quietly, a small but distinctive wobble in my voice betraying my hurt. "See you tomorrow night, Finn, if you're still able to come."

Before he can say anything, I turn and give Maisie her "Forward" instruction, hoping that Poppy gets the message I don't fancy walking together right now and hangs back a bit.

"Ella, hey," River says, catching up with me once I've walked a few paces. "Is it OK if I walk this way with you?"

"Go ahead," I mutter glumly, unable to shake my frustration from my previous conversation.

"I was waiting until you finished chatting with your sister. I didn't want to interrupt. It looked … uh … intense. Should we wait for her? I think she's still talking to Finn."

"It's fine," I say, as Maisie and I continue down the pavement.

"I'm excited to come to your house tomorrow! Thanks so much for inviting me. *Doctor Who* is already one of my favourite TV shows, but I reckon watching it with other people is going to make it even better. That way we can talk about it!"

"Finn will happily chat through the whole episode, trust me."

I'm hit with a wave of sadness that River talks like he's used to watching things alone.

"What time do you want me to come over?" he asks eagerly.

"I'm around all day so you can come whenever."

An idea pops into my head. It could be a bad one,

but I decide to take the risk. I bring Maisie to a stop so I can turn to face River properly.

"River, are you, by any chance, interested in mythology?" I ask cautiously.

"Mythology?" He sounds a bit thrown by the random question, but happily he goes with it. "Yeah! You mean like gods and legends and stuff? Sure, who isn't interested in that? A lot of cool stories. And scary ones."

"I know this may seem a bit odd, but if you're free tomorrow morning, would you be up for coming to the Mythos Library with me and Maisie?"

"The Mythos Library," he repeats slowly. "Isn't that a museum?"

"Yeah, I know that sounds boring. Not exactly how you'd want to spend your Saturday. You know what, it's a stupid idea, forget that I—"

"No, I'd love to come," he cuts in, sounding sincere. "I don't know much about mythology, though. I'd need a lot explaining to me."

"That's OK," I say, breaking into a grin. "I happen to know someone."

CHAPTER SIX

When we arrive at the Mythos Library the next morning, it's heaving with crowds, which is different to when Maisie and I first came here on a school trip not too long ago.

Ailynn herself has admitted that she was never good at publicity, so it was no wonder that, when our teacher Mr Wilson organized the school visit, the place was deserted, and no one had even heard of it. Apart from Finn, of course. If he's not spending time with animals then he usually has his nose stuck in a book about mythology, and no one was more excited for that school trip than him. I felt lucky that day to have not one but *two* tour guides: Finn and Ailynn described all the artefacts and stories behind them in amazing detail.

We didn't know then that Ailynn was hiding a big secret: that she was a descendant of Sunsight, the keeper first charged with watching over Lugh, who remained trapped in a chest deep underground two millennia later. She was devastated that he escaped on her watch, even though it wasn't her fault. Everett Croft knocked her unconscious so she wouldn't get in the way of his evil plans. It was at her request that Maisie, Finn, Poppy and I set out to find the rainbow stones to beat him. Since then, we've stayed close friends. It's hard not to be when you're all bound by the same secret.

It also helped that, when Dad's publicity business dropped Everett, its biggest client, he was on the hunt for a new project. I made certain that the Mythos Library was on his radar and he leaped at the chance to help someone as kind and hardworking as Ailynn to make her small business a success. Thanks to him and his team, the Mythos Library has had a complete rebrand with a glitzy launch party and everything.

"Listen to what this reviewer calls it," Dad had announced to us the day after the party. "She says that the Mythos Library is 'a beautiful hidden gem which conjures mythological magic in every room, no legend or story left untold. With a vast collection of artefacts and run by a woman who will leave you in awe of her mythical knowledge, this museum is unmissable.' You hear that? *Unmissable!* Hopefully, this will bring in some bookings."

It did. As did all the other reviews. Soon, the Mythos Library was considered one of *the* places to visit in London, and Ailynn suddenly found herself having to quickly hire staff to help keep up with the heaps of admin while conducting all the tours herself.

While he may have spruced up the branding, Dad's been careful not to mess with the charm of the museum itself – as soon as we turned down the street from the main road earlier, I recognized the creaking of the old wooden sign that hangs off the building's wall.

"There's such a cool atmosphere to this place," River says as we step into the museum. "It sounds weird, but it's like I can *feel* the history and the stories of it."

"That doesn't sound weird," I assure him. "I felt the same when I first came here. I think Maisie did, too. We could sense something was … different about this museum."

It's probably best not to mention that I soon

discovered that was because there was a Celtic god being held hostage in the ground beneath it.

When Mum and I met River this morning to make our way to the Mythos Library together, I worried that I'd made a mistake in inviting him. I knew I would have to speak honestly about what happened on the Day of Darkness to Ailynn, and I wasn't sure if River was going to freak out about it all. But when we had to get on the tube, I was so grateful he was there as well as Mum.

I rely heavily on Maisie to guide me on public transport and I know I can trust her, but it's still a daunting experience and having a friend to keep my spirits up is always a major bonus. The London Underground is a loud, busy maze with challenges and obstacles that pop up out of nowhere. As we got to the station, I instructed Maisie to "Find the lift", so she knew to take me to the nearest elevator down to the underground, but River was able to tell me that it was out of order, so we made our way to the escalator. I'm less confident on those, but Maisie was brilliant, and thanks to Mum helping me and River chatting normally when I needed distraction and let me focus when I neared the end, I didn't feel like I was in the way, holding everyone up. And, once Maisie led me to a seat, River made me laugh on the train, his light conversation easing my worries. Thanks to him, Mum and Maisie, the journey to the Mythos Library was fun. Mum wanted to go to a nearby department store to pick up a few things, so she dropped us off at the museum and is meeting us back here in an hour.

"This museum goes up *forever*," River comments, gasping as we reach the bottom of the stairs. "There are so many floors!"

"Yeah, it's tall. The artefacts on display here cover a lot of different mythologies."

"Whoa. We have a lot of ground to cover."

"The main reason I wanted to come today was to speak to the curator, Ailynn. Do you see her anywhere? She's got long blonde hair, a nose piercing and a sun tattoo on her wrist. She usually guides the tours, but I can't hear any taking place at the moment."

"No, she doesn't seem to be on this floor. We could try the others?"

"Guess so. Let's keep going up until we find her."

Finding the banister, I tell Maisie to "Step stand" – her instruction to stand on the first step so I can work out how high it is – before we begin the climb up and round the winding staircase. We pause on the landing of each floor so River can tell me if he sees anyone matching Ailynn's description, but we still haven't found her by the time we reach Greek mythology at the top.

"This is so strange," I tell River, frowning as he leads me to a corner out of the way of the bustling crowds moving slowly round each artefact. "Whenever I've come here before she's been *somewhere* in the building. Are you sure she's not leading the tour group you mentioned?"

"Definitely not her," he says in a hushed voice, as the group in question files out of the room, making their way down to the next section. "The person leading that is a young guy with brown hair. He looks nervous. I'd say this is his first tour group."

"That makes sense. Ailynn usually does the tours. It was something she was passionate about holding on to when the museum took off with bookings. The staff she hired were mostly to take over the office side of things and to help visitors with general questions."

"Maybe she's on a break or in a meeting? We could ask someone. There's a member of staff on the other side of the room. Shall I go ask them if they know where she is?"

"Yes please. Thanks, River. If they could let her

know that I'm here to talk to her, that would be great," I say, smiling gratefully. "Then while we wait for her, we should enjoy the museum. Are you happy to start on this floor with Greek mythology?"

"Probably the best place for me to start, since I don't know much about the others," he says, sounding embarrassed. "At least I've heard of some of these legends. OK, back soon."

He walks off, the creak of his footsteps across the wonky wooden floorboards fading as he makes his way to the other side of the room.

"Excuse me," a woman says shyly to me while I wait, "do you need any help at all?"

"Oh, no, thank you, I'm waiting for my friend."

"OK, good, I saw you standing here and I wanted to check."

"Thank you so much, I appreciate that," I gush, a warmth filling my stomach.

"Enjoy the museum, so many wonderful things," she says cheerfully, before I hear her stroll out the room and down the stairs.

After such a small gesture from a stranger, I feel a couple of inches taller. It puts me in a sunshiny positive mood, and when River returns, I'm beaming at him.

"I spoke to a woman who works here and she said that the last few days, whenever Ailynn has come into work she's gone straight into her office and stayed in there until late, barely speaking to anyone," River tells me, concern lacing his words. "Is that normal for her?"

My good mood vanishes in an instant. I feel anxious and on edge.

"No!"

"I didn't think so from what you've already told me. Anyway, she's gone downstairs to tell Ailynn that we're here and she says she'll come find us once she's spoken to her."

I nod. Part of me hoped that coming here would quash my silly gut instinct. I wanted Ailynn to laugh at my theory that the unbearable noise might be connected to the Eye of Horus. I wanted to be able to go home and be as confused as everyone else until someone officially explained what was happening. I guess a part of me hoped that, this time, it would be up to someone else to work out how to save the day.

But now Ailynn is acting strangely, too, that hope is fading.

"While we wait, shall we—"

River's sentence trails off and an unease twists my

72

stomach into knots as my pendant grows hot and I hear the noise.

"Oh no," he whispers, terrified.

Just like before, the noise starts out like a background hum of different unpleasant sounds, enough to prompt a chorus of gasps and yelps to erupt throughout the building. We all know what's coming. It grows louder, roaring in my ears, flooding every sense. As I feel the Eye of Horus growing warm on my skin, its power sending ripples of calm through my body, I instinctively reach for River. I've barely touched him but he wrenches his arm away from me in anger, his hands flying up to cover his ears.

"River, deep breaths," I say urgently, trying to find him again but it's no use – he won't let me near him. "River, can you hear my voice? *Please*, try to listen to me."

I hear him thud back against the wall as he slides down to sit, whimpering at first and then yelling and screaming like everyone else. The room descends into a shouting match. Friends and families explode into arguments, blaming each other for what's happening, finding any excuse to complain. I crouch down with Maisie and throw an arm round her as she nuzzles into me. She's not affected by the noise, but she can sense the fear clouding the room. I hear someone's yell of frustration, followed by a loud *clunk*, as though they've loosened something heavy from its stand. My mind races with possible explanations, knowing that the antiquities are safely encased in glass cabinets, before it strikes me that there is something else that's heavy in this room which could be picked up: I think they might be wielding the fire extinguisher.

"Please don't do what I think you might d—"

My frantic request is interrupted by a deafening *smash*. I hear the glass of one of the cases crack loudly and I gasp, clasping a hand over my mouth.

The unbearable noise stops.

I exhale with relief, my breath shaky and uneven.

"Did you try to break into this case?" someone cries.

"I wasn't thinking," their companion replies hastily, putting down what I think must be the fire extinguisher with a gentle thud on the ground. "You weren't listening to my point. You were yelling over me and I had to somehow—"

"You were shouting at me! That's it. I'm leaving."

Their reckless exchange isn't out of the norm here. Everyone in the room is having the same fight, all of them furious. The noise has gone, but the loud rage remains.

"River, are you OK?" I ask, reaching out carefully towards him.

But the moment I touch his arm, he pulls away sharply.

"Don't touch me!" he snaps.

"OK, sorry. Take your time," I say gently, standing up and feeling for the wall behind me so I can lean back and have a moment to catch my breath.

My stomach churning, I hear a voice carrying up the stairs over the din of various arguments: "Ella! Ella? Where are you?"

"Ailynn!" I cry back, straightening, but I'm not sure she can hear me.

"Ella, if you can hear me, come down here to the ground floor when you can!"

"Did you hear that, River?" I ask him. "We need to go downstairs. River?"

"Yes, I hear you," he says, sounding tired and defeated. "I'm … taking a moment."

I reach out to place my hand on his arm and this time he doesn't pull away. River lets me silently comfort him to the background noise of everyone else in the room arguing.

CHAPTER SEVEN

"As soon as it happened, I thought it might be Homados," Ailynn tells us a few minutes later when we're tucked away in her office, as her staff close the museum for the day and help to safely escort all visitors out. "It was the battle noise in the distance. It was disguised with all the other horrible sounds, but it was there. I heard it."

I take a sip of the steaming cup of tea Ailynn made for me. Maisie is under my feet and River is next to me, having barely said a word since the noise faded away. He seems much more affected than the last time it happened. Mum called straight away to check we were OK and once I'd reassured her we were fine, I told her we'd wait in Ailynn's office until she could make her way back to the museum.

There are two reasons why Ailynn has been holed up in her office recently. Firstly, she broke her ankle on a rock-climbing weekend in Wales a week ago, which she embarked on in her newfound spirit of "living life to the full", having felt rocked by the events of Lugh and the Day of Darkness. Secondly, she's been researching everything there is to know about Homados, the god of tumult and din, the god she believes is responsible for all of this.

"I-I heard the battle noise loudly this time," River stammers. He gulps audibly. "It felt like I was in the middle of the battle itself, and the only way out was to scream and shout. It felt so unnatural. It was horrible."

"That's how you're meant to feel," Ailynn tells him softly. "It's not only you, River. Everyone feels that way when they hear it. It's not your fault."

He doesn't say anything.

"Ailynn, who is Homados?" I ask.

"A god from Greek mythology," she says, her chair squeaking as she leans back in it. "As I mentioned to you, he's the god of battle noise and tumult. Homados specializes in the angry, confused shouts of men and the clashing of weapons."

77

"That's what I can hear," I say, my heart thumping against my chest. "*That's* the noise."

"Yes, unbearable, isn't it. A nasty element of war. It's a din that overwhelms and brings unease and restlessness." She pauses to sigh. "I thought that I'd jumped to conclusions at first, thinking it was him. I figured that I was still wrestling with everything that had happened on the Day of Darkness and that I was overthinking it."

"You're not the only one who has felt like that," I assure her, and a weight that's been hanging over my heart lifts ever so slightly. I move to put my mug down on her desk, sweeping my hand left and right, feeling for the coaster, and touching the base of the mug down slowly so it's placed correctly on to it. "I need to tell you something, Ailynn. When the noise happens, the Eye of Horus … helps me."

She gasps. "Are you sure?"

"Yes. I can feel it getting warm as though something has been switched on inside it and then I can feel the rage from the noise fade away to inner calmness."

"Oh, Ella, this is *brilliant*," she says enthusiastically, taking me by surprise. "I mean, not brilliant, obviously none of this is good. But the Eye of Horus protects from the work of gods, and if it's working against this then that confirms this *is* an act of a god. It's Homados, I know it. According to legends, he can mutter incantations that cause awful noise and he can make it spread far and wide. He must be casting the spell over the whole world at whim!"

I hear her chair squeak again as she moves to get up, and the clack of her crutches as she uses them to cross her office, followed by the sound of books shifting along a shelf. She says, "Here we are. It's all in this book," and pulls a volume off the shelf that's obviously big and heavy as she emits a small "*Oof*" as she retrieves it, carrying it over to her desk. There's a soft thud as she puts it down, before I hear her plonk herself back in her chair again and the sound of her flicking through the book, looking for a specific page.

River emits a small cough as she busies herself. "I'm sorry, but … are you two talking about a god from Greek mythology being behind this? As in, a god that's … real?"

"Yes, we are, sorry, I should have given some context before bringing you here," I say, deciding there's no point in trying to hide it. We need answers now. "The Day of Darkness was caused by a Celtic god called Lugh who was spurred on by Everett

Croft to steal the light from the world. Poppy, Finn, Maisie and I helped Lugh give the light back. It's a long story."

There's a beat of silence broken only by Ailynn turning another page.

"Oh, and Lugh gave me a pendant," I add hurriedly. "You know, the necklace I'm always wearing. It's called the Eye of Horus and it protects me from the dangers of gods."

I hear River exhale a shaky breath before he slowly says, "*OK…*"

"Ailynn, what do you think Homados wants? Why is he doing this?" I ask, getting back to the point and giving River time to get his head around that brief overview of events. "And how can we make it stop?"

"Here, this is the chapter I was after," she says, her voice low and cautious. "This book centres around long-lost ancient artefacts of the mythological world and their place in legend. There is a little-known story about Homados, a rumour about something he's always wanted. The legend goes that he hunts for ultimate power over men and gods by throwing the world into chaos and using the Shield of Hercules to defend himself from threat."

"The Shield of Hercules," I repeat. "I haven't heard of it."

"Finn might have," she says warmly, one of Finn's biggest fans since they developed a bond during the events of the Day of Darkness when she was impressed by his extensive mythological knowledge and enthusiasm. "There's a famous poem about it and it describes the depiction of Homados on the shield itself, along with various elements of war symbolized by other gods. The shield is almost completely unbeatable."

"No wonder Homados wants it."

"I'd say it's next on his list," she remarks nervously. "He's already begun to wreak havoc on the world with the noise. You know the only way to find relief from that? To be angry yourself. To shout and scream and hate. Our rage is the only way to drown out the pain and din of the unbearable noise. That's what it says in this book anyway."

"And that's what's happening out there, Ailynn. I can hear it while I'm protected by the pendant. I can hear everyone turning on one another, even people they love." I run my fingers through my hair, pushing it back from my face. "This is the work of Homados, I'm sure of it now."

"Everything that's happening does seem to match the legend," Ailynn reasons.

"And we know that not all legend is myth," I point out, thinking back on my adventures with Lugh. "Before Lugh escaped, you told me a story about what would happen if he did. We all lived that story."

"In which case, Ella, I feel the need to warn you about something very important in Homados's story," she says gravely. "The Shield of Hercules has been lost for centuries. Folklore tells us that Zeus realized the extent of its power, how it could be turned against fellow gods – make one of them invincible to the others – and so he instructed Hermes to hide it somewhere. He knew what could happen if it landed in the wrong hands."

"You mean, with someone like Homados?"

"Exactly. Hermes did as he was told, and according to legend, he created a map, the Carta Atlantia, otherwise known as the Map of Movement. It is designed to test its reader with a series of challenges. Hermes is a trickster god, as I'm sure you know—"

"Uh, right, yeah, course," I lie.

"And so he made it personal. Supposedly, the map takes its reader where they need to go, but really it takes you to the place you fear the most."

"That's … mean," I say weakly.

"Hermes never cared about being all that nice, although he has his moments," Ailynn remarks. "The map is accompanied by his compass."

"Whose compass?"

"The compass of Hermes. It belongs with the map. Neither will work without the other." She pauses. "Which leads me on to a point about the shield. I believe it's … incomplete."

"Sorry?"

"I've read that Hermes buried the shield in one place, and then took the key to it somewhere else," she explains.

"How can a shield have a key?" River asks in confusion, and I perk up at him getting involved. He must be confused right now, but at least he's still here.

I wouldn't have blamed him if he'd wanted to run away before now. This is a lot to take in.

"According to the *Almanac of Curious Myths* –" I hear Ailynn flick through the pages of a book – "right in the middle of the shield, in the centre of all the depictions of war, is a small dent in the shape of … an eye. An eye that symbolizes what a shield must do, which is protect its holder," she concludes quietly.

My mouth feels very dry. "The shield offers

protection from the gods," I whisper, trying not to panic. *Deep breath in. Deep breath out. Deep breath in. Deep breath—*

"Ailynn, is Homados coming after the Eye of Horus?"

"Maybe," she says, sounding pained.

"As in, the Eye of Horus pendant that Ella is wearing," River squeaks, his voice a few pitches higher than normal. "*That* Eye of Horus?"

"There's only one," Ailynn confirms as fear begins to seep through every bone in my body and turn it to ice. "We can't know any of this for sure, Ella. I could be completely wrong. Maybe this isn't Homados at all! Maybe it's a corporation or aliens or monsters or … whatever social media says it is." She hesitates. "Although, the timing fits."

"What do you mean?" I ask urgently.

"I've been wondering why Homados would do this now, if it was him. Then I realized that he knew Lugh had the Eye of Horus. Lugh won it fair and square – a great story, but one for another day. My point is, Homados would know by now that Lugh has escaped from his prison. He would have heard it on the grapevine … or *god*-vine, if you will."

She forces a laugh. Neither me nor River join in.

Maisie sighs with disappointment. Ailynn clears her throat.

"Anyway," she continues, flustered, "he will know that Lugh has given it away. Perhaps Homados knows Lugh gave it to someone here on earth and that's why he's put his plan into play."

I sit back in my chair, goosebumps covering my skin.

"He's coming for me," I surmise.

"I don't think Lugh would have given it to you if he'd known of Homados's plan," Ailynn says hurriedly. "If this is his plan at all."

"It is. The Eye of Horus has been warning me."

I bite my lip. It's surreal, the idea of owning an item that a powerful god is searching for. I think over everything that Ailynn has told me today, replaying the story in my head, matching it to all the events that have happened so far. The whole time, my gut instincts are telling me what I need to do.

I ignore it for as long as possible until I can't any more.

"Homados, god of battle noise and tumult, wants to become the most powerful god there is and throw the world into chaos," I begin.

"The more unbearable noise he feeds us, the

angrier we get to make it stop," Ailynn says. "It won't be long before fighting breaks out everywhere. It could even lead to war."

"And then he'll take control of us all and no one will be able to stop him because he'll have the Shield of Hercules, which protects him against the other gods."

"Yes, but remember, the shield must be complete with the Eye of Horus to work. Otherwise, it's hopeless," Ailynn points out.

"The Eye of Horus that I have."

"Yes."

"OK, right. OK," I repeat, willing myself to be braver as I twirl the pendant absent-mindedly through my fingers.

Maisie nudges my ankle with her cold wet nose.

I'm here, she's saying. *You don't have to pretend to be brave with me.*

I breathe out all the air in my cheeks and then give a sharp, decided nod.

"Then there's only one thing to do," I announce, sounding much more confident than I feel. "I'll have to find the shield before he does."

CHAPTER EIGHT

"No," Ailynn says in disbelief. "*No*, Ella."

"Do you know where it is?" I ask, ignoring her protests. "Oh wait, you said Hermes hid it somewhere that would be personal to the map reader. So I have to find the Map of Movement and the compass that goes with that first, right? They'll lead me to the shield. I'm guessing Homados hasn't found any of these yet, otherwise the noise would be constant. He won't want the gods getting wind of his plan and coming to stop him before he's ready. I wonder where they could—"

"Now, h-hold on a minute," Ailynn interjects as I ramble on to myself, mostly from the nerves that are sending adrenaline coursing through my body. "You can't be serious."

"I *am* serious. How else are we going to stop him?"

"I don't know!" she cries. "But we're talking about a very powerful god here. He's not the god of flowers! Or the god of love or kindness, or the god of music! He's the god of battle noise and tumult."

I frown. "*Is* there a god of flowers? I didn't know that. Sounds like a nice gig."

"Ella," Ailynn says through gritted teeth, brushing aside my hopeless attempt to lighten the mood, "I didn't tell you this story only for you to think that it meant you needed to somehow get involved."

"I know that."

"Last time, I had to lie in a hospital bed, knowing that I'd sent a twelve-year-old girl on what seemed to be an impossible mission! That's not happening again. Especially with my leg in this state. I wouldn't be able to come with you!"

"But the last mission wasn't impossible. I did it," I say. Then I correct myself. "*We* did it – Poppy, Finn, Maisie and me. You told me it was my destiny and I believed you, remember?"

"How could I forget?!"

"Then believe me now when I say to you that something is telling me that I can't sit back and wait for whatever is coming. I think I'm meant to be part of this. Lugh gave *me* the pendant, remember." I hesitate before adding, "I don't think this is someone else's story – I think this is mine."

She doesn't say anything, not for a few moments. In the hope that I'm starting to sway her, I quickly ask my burning question: "Ailynn, do you know where the map and compass belonging to Hermes are?"

"Yes," she admits.

"Where? Where can I find them?"

"In the private collection of a wealthy owner who lives just outside of London. I don't think he realizes what he has," she reveals reluctantly. "They don't work without the Eye of Horus. The map will seem like a … blank piece of parchment. And the compass, like a round gold paperweight. Ever since their discovery was announced, I've had my suspicions of what they might be. This collector knows they're important, he just doesn't know why."

"If I take them, then they should work for me because I have the Eye of Horus?"

"I imagine so." She sounds tired and deflated.

"Do you have his name and address?" I ask.

"Ella, it won't be easy getting these items. He won't simply hand them over. They'll be well-protected by security. And I don't know how to emphasize this more, but once you have the map, it will not be an easy journey. Do you understand?"

"I've faced difficult journeys before."

"Not like this." She hesitates before continuing in a low, apprehensive voice. "Have you ever felt trapped in a nightmare, utterly powerless to the fear and horror closing in on you? The ones that leave you drenched in sweat and screaming as you wake up? Imagine that but with no chance of waking up. You can't escape these challenges once you're in them."

"Ailynn—"

"This quest is designed individually for whoever reads the map, everything will be created around *your* fears, *your* worst nightmares," she says urgently, desperately trying to get across the seriousness of the conversation. "Hermes will want to test your conviction, but also your heart. He won't give up the shield willingly. You may have to face demons, both mythological and … personal."

I nod slowly. "I know. I'm ready."

"You're *not* ready for this, Ella."

Swallowing, I reach out to place my hand on Maisie's fur. "I'll never forget how scared I was when I first held the guide-dog harness. I stood still for so long, too afraid to take the first step. But somehow, I managed to find the courage to put one foot forward. That was all I had to do – put one foot in front of the other. Then, I took another step, and then another until I got to where I needed to be. The hardest bit is starting the journey, right?"

Ailynn sighs.

"I believe that I can do this, Ailynn," I tell her confidently. "I know it's going to be hard, and I know that I'm going to … struggle at times. But I also think I'm determined enough to have a chance of winning. That's half the battle, don't you think? Believing you have a shot."

"Oh goodness," she groans, relenting. "You really are going to do this, aren't you. I shouldn't let this happen. This stupid injury! It shouldn't be you who has to go. *I* should do this. I should be the one to stop Homados. I'm the grown-up here."

"No, it has to be me. I'm not affected by the noise thanks to the pendant."

"I know I'm slow at the moment, but I could try to do it. You could always give the pendant to me to do this mission and then I'll give it right back."

I break into a smile. I know she's being truthful and not trying to trick me.

"Thanks Ailynn, but Lugh gave it to me for a

reason," I remind her. "He didn't give it to me so I could give it away when things got tough. I know better than anyone that when things are at their darkest, you need to trust yourself to find the light. No one else can do that for you. Sorry, Ailynn, but it *has* to be me who does this."

She sighs then chuckles softly. "You know what, Ella? Although this idea goes against every sensible thought in my head, I think you might be right. If anyone can do this, it's you." She sits back down again and types at her keyboard. "Let me find the collector's address. Remember, if you get the map and it's blank, don't be put off. It will work for the reader worthy of it wearing the Eye of Horus."

"Got it." I reach down to stroke Maisie's head. "I guess now all I have to do is work out how to get past this collector's security to borrow such priceless items."

"Actually, Ella," River begins timidly, "I think I might be able to help with that."

For the whole journey to his house, River is very quiet.

I want to be patient and give him time to process the whole mythological-gods-are-real thing until he's ready to talk about it, and it's not like we can talk about it in front of Mum anyway. But when she's dropped us off safely at his gate and we have a bit of adult-free time, I decide to check whether he has any questions.

"River, are you OK? Do you want to discuss what you've just heard? You know, the stuff about the … gods and the Day of Darkness and … well, everything. You probably think that it's a joke or that Ailynn and I were making strange things up!"

"If I thought that, I wouldn't have offered to help."

I pause. "Yeah, OK, but –" I frown – "aren't you, I don't know … shocked?"

He snorts. "Ella, this morning I found out that mythological gods do *exist* and that my new friend saved the world from them once and now has to do it again. So, yes, I'm definitely shocked."

"Then, why aren't you asking me lots of questions? Why aren't you demanding answers? Why are you still friends with me?" I ask, throwing my hand up.

"Because I believe you," he says simply.

"You do? Are you sure?"

"Yes. I mean, it took me a minute in Ailynn's office, but it all makes sense. And listening to what you were both saying and how you were talking –" he takes a deep breath – "I could tell you were scared. She was too. You can't fake that. I don't think anyone could have been in there and not believed you. So, even if it's all a bit strange, I want to help. And it didn't sound as though we had the time for me to panic about it."

I can't help but grin at him. "That's true. We don't."

"OK, so I help you and then, when you've got the shield or whatever it is you need to stop that unbearable noise, I can bombard you with zillions of questions then."

"Sounds like a plan. Right, shall we go into your house? Tell me what it's like."

"We're currently at the gate at the end of the driveway to my house, which is a big modern glass building that looks as though it was designed by a *James Bond* villain."

I laugh as he puts in the code to the gate, letting it swing open automatically before we walk down the long gravel driveway to his house, pebbles crunching beneath our feet. When we get to his front door, I hear all these beeps and the swish of a door sweeping open as it unlocks via another code he's punched into a keypad that he tells me is built into the wall. It definitely *sounds* like the house has all the security a *Bond* villain might have.

Maisie and I step inside. When he shuts the door behind us, the noise of it closing echoes, the reverberations taking a while to fade.

This space must be big with high ceilings.

"The whole of this floor is open-plan," River murmurs, sounding a little embarrassed. "So we're standing in the hallway, but the kitchen is to our right and the drawing and dining room is to the left, with no doors or walls separating anything. The drawing room side leads out to the garden; the walls are all glass. Straight ahead of us running parallel to the back wall is the staircase, which has no banister. And in terms of decoration … uh … well, there is none. My parents are very into minimalist design."

"Wow! Sounds amazing."

"Not so fun to live in, though. Growing up in a glass cube is a bit limiting. No mess allowed and lots of sharp corners. Cold and pristine. But, hey, it looks cool," he adds bitterly.

"Are your parents at home?" I ask, steering the conversation away from the design.

"Nope. They don't come home much. I think they're in France at the moment."

"But you can't live here by yourself?"

"I don't. Irving looks after me mostly."

"Who's Irving?"

My question is answered by the sound of shoes clacking across the floor towards me, and then a man's voice I don't recognize bounces off the walls.

"Good afternoon, sir, and welcome home," he says in a clipped, posh tone. "I trust your outing to the museum went well?"

"Irving, please don't call me 'sir'," River groans. "I've asked you so many times."

"My apologies, *River*," Irving says, although he sounds distinctly uncomfortable.

"Thanks. And yes, the museum was … interesting." River clears his throat. "This is my friend Ella, who I've told you about, and her guide dog, Maisie."

"A pleasure to meet you both. My name is Irving. I'm River's butler."

"*Guardian*," River corrects through a hiss. "You're more like a guardian."

"If you like," Irving says, but, again, he doesn't sound too pleased.

"You have a butler?" I gasp in amazement. "That's awesome!"

"He's my parents' butler," River says hurriedly. "And like I say, he's in charge of taking care of me when they're away. It's like having a big brother, sort of. Just one who cooks for you and drives you places and sorts your laundry and … uh … looks after the house."

Irving clears his throat. "May I offer you and your guests some refreshments?"

"Ella, do you want a drink?" River translates.

"Sure! What do you have?"

There's a pause, before Irving says, "Everything, Miss Jones."

"*Everything?*"

"Everything. Is there a fruit juice to which you are partial? For example: orange, pineapple, apple, mango, grape, grapefruit, beetroot, carrot, strawberry, tomato, pomegranate – or a mixture of two or more? Perhaps you'd like a sparkling drink of some kind? We have all the major brands and flavours, as well as several lesser-known independent manufacturers. If you'd rather a tea, we have all the usual suspects: black, green, white, oolong, herbal, Pu-Erh, flower or fruit. We can also offer you coffee any way you'd like – Americano, cappuccino, macchiato, mocha, espresso, latte, iced – and you can let me know if there's a specific coffee bean you'd prefer, whether that be Colombian or—"

"Thanks, Irving, I think she's got the idea," River interrupts, sounding flustered.

"Uh, yeah, wow, thanks, Irving," I say, a little overwhelmed at the options and weirdly exhausted after listening to them. "I'll just have water."

If my choice is a disappointment to Irving, he doesn't let on. Instead he says, "Still or sparkling?"

"Still, thanks."

"Any particular brand you'd like? We have—"

"We'll have two glasses of whatever water you pick for us," River cuts in before Irving can rattle yet more options off. "And a bowl of water for Maisie, thanks."

"At once," Irving says. "Can I offer you a—"

His sentence is cut short by a loud blaring siren that goes off through the entire house, making me jump.

"That's the intruder alarm," Irving declares, raising his voice over the noise. "I'd better check the CCTV. May I recommend that you and Miss Jones make your way to the safe room immediately, sir."

"Don't call me sir," River says sharply. "And there's no need to check the CCTV. The intruders have climbed over the wall and jumped down this side into the garden. I can see who it is from here. Don't worry, Irving – you can go turn off the alarm."

"Wait, you can see who is breaking in?" I ask, panicked. "How come you're so calm?"

"Because I know them, and so do you," he tells me. "It's Poppy and Finn."

CHAPTER NINE

"What were you *thinking*?" I demand to know from Poppy and Finn once Irving has turned off the alarm and River has opened the front door to call them inside. "Why would you break into River's house?"

"We didn't plan on breaking in," Finn says weakly.

"In my defence, I did try to open the gate first," Poppy says haughtily. "I put in, like, ten different codes before we decided to climb the wall."

"Even if you'd guessed the code, that would still be breaking in! Why didn't you ring the bell?" I ask.

"We thought we'd check the place out first before letting you know we were here," she reasons. "No offence, River, but your house looks like it belongs to a supervillain. A cool, mega-wealthy supervillain with great taste in architecture who probably has a huge TikTok following, but a supervillain all the same."

"*Poppy*," I hiss, my cheeks burning with embarrassment.

"I said it looks more like Tony Stark's house in the *Iron Man* films," Finn says quickly. "So not necessarily the house of a supervillain. It could be the house of a superhero."

I'm relieved when I hear River laugh.

I put a hand on my hip. "What are you two even doing here in the first place? I thought you had the second round of the tennis tournament, Poppy. And you're meant to be helping Meg with the lion cubs aren't you, Finn?"

"We realized that we maybe hadn't been as supportive as we could have been, Ella," Finn admits. "Last night, I couldn't sleep. I kept thinking about what you'd said about how if there was any way that this horrible noise could be linked to –" he hesitates, unaware of who in this room knows what – "*you know*, then you wanted to do all you could to stop it. I realized you were right and that it was worth checking out. I'm sorry I didn't trust you at the time."

My expression softens. "Thanks, Finn."

Poppy sniffs. "And my tournament has been

cancelled until things are a bit more normal or whatever. But I also thought that *maybe* you were on to something."

"I appreciate the support, Poppy. That still doesn't exactly explain what you were doing breaking into River's house."

"OK, we weren't breaking in, we were *scoping* the place out. Big difference," Poppy maintains huffily. "By the time Finn and I realized that maybe we'd like to come along to the Mythos Library, too, you were already there and then the noise happened."

"That delayed us a bit," Finn adds. "By the time we got to Ailynn, she told us that you two had left and she mentioned you were coming to River's house to get some supplies for the … uh … mission."

"Maybe we should talk about this in my room," River suggests.

"Shall I bring refreshments upstairs?" Irving checks.

"No thanks, we'll come down in a bit."

"Very well, sir— I mean, *River*."

"Whoa," Poppy says, impressed. "Your dad is super formal, River."

"This isn't my dad," River mumbles.

"I'm the family butler," Irving clarifies.

Poppy gasps. "Wait, what? You have a *butler*?"

"We'll be upstairs, Irving," River presses in a strained voice, desperate to move on from this situation. I hear his footsteps retreat to the back of the room. "Come on, let's go."

"You go ahead," Poppy says, and I feel her hand gently wrap around my wrist as she stops me before I can give Maisie her command to move forward. "Ella, those stairs have no banister, they're a bit intense. I'll stick with you to make sure you get up carefully."

"Thanks," I say, as River and Finn lead the way.

It's not until I hear their voices grow quieter as they head up and Poppy grips my hand tighter, coming to stand in front of me head on that I realize Poppy is waiting for them to be out of earshot so she can speak to me.

"Are you OK?" I ask, confused. "What's going on?"

"I could ask you the same questions!" she says in a low, hushed voice. "Ella, do you think it's the right thing to do to bring River in on all this?"

I shake my hand free of her grip. "What are you talking about?"

"We barely know him. After everything that we went through on the Day of Darkness, do you think it's a good idea to have someone come along who we've only just met? If this Homados-god-person is real, then River doesn't know what he's getting himself into."

"Up until just now, you didn't think it was anything to do with the gods at all."

"That's not true, I said I wasn't *sure*," she says defensively. "Ailynn was convincing."

"River didn't need Ailynn to convince him to come with me this morning."

"That's not fair, Ella, he didn't know *why* you were going to the museum. Ailynn told us that he had no idea about any of it. She said he was so shocked he barely spoke!"

"It's a lot to take in. Not many people would believe it."

She hesitates, lowering her voice even more. "That's the other thing. Why does he believe it so easily? Shouldn't he have heard Ailynn's story and run away screaming? That would be a normal person's reaction."

"I don't remember you running away screaming when Ailynn was lying in the hospital bed, telling us that the world had gone dark because the Celtic god of light was getting his vengeance on mankind."

"All the light had gone from the world, Ella! It wasn't a stretch to think there was something magical going on," she huffs.

"And now the whole world is tormented by battle noise that creates rage and disharmony," I hiss back at her. "You don't think there's something magical about that?"

"Yeah, I do now! But I've met Lugh. I know now that a lot of the mythological stories and legends might be true!"

"But yesterday when it was a toss-up between the Mythos Museum and your tennis tournament, you didn't think it could be connected."

"Maybe I didn't *want* to believe it, Ella," she snaps, her sharp tone taking me aback. "Maybe I was scared to."

I don't know what to say to that. I can hear her unsteady breathing, fast and shallow from her flare of anger.

"Poppy—" I begin, but a voice upstairs calls out to us, interrupting.

"Everything OK?" Finn says. "Are you two coming? You'll never believe this!"

"We'll be right there," Poppy calls back, before addressing me coldly. "After you."

I give Maisie a "Forward" instruction. Poppy trails after us in silence, waiting as we reach the stairs and I tell Maisie to "Step stand", letting her put her front paws on the first step. Despite the tension still lingering between us, Poppy insists on helping me up the stairs since there's no handrail I can hold on to.

The sound of our footsteps echoes through the house. Neither of us say a word.

I'm annoyed at her implying that she doesn't want River in on this with us, and wonder if that's jealousy because I'm getting close to someone else. That wouldn't be fair of her. She's been so busy with her sports training, it's not like we've been hanging out together. I've got the impression she hasn't had time to miss me. It's nice to have a new friend.

But I didn't consider that the reason Poppy was reluctant to believe me straight away about the Eye of Horus was because she was scared of what that might mean.

That, I can understand.

"In here!" Finn calls out, his voice floating down the landing to the right when we've reached the top of the staircase. "We're in River's room."

When we step into his bedroom, I hear Poppy gasp behind me.

"This cannot be your room, River," she says in total awe. "It's the size of our house!"

"Slight exaggeration," Finn chuckles, coming to stand next to me. "Ella, the room is big with dark walls and some cool modern art—"

"My parents chose that," River interjects irritably. "I wanted to hang some posters but they said it might mark the paint and would ruin the vibe of the house."

"You've got a king-size bed to your left with square bedside tables either side," Finn continues excitedly. "The walk-in wardrobe is to the left of the bed, and to your right you have the en-suite bathroom through the first door, and through the second door … well, that's where you can take over, River. It's incredible."

"What is it?" I ask, intrigued as Maisie and I make our way across the room to this mysterious second door.

"Can we talk about this walk-in wardrobe?" Poppy cries as she goes to examine it. "River, you have your own shop!"

"My dad's friend is in the fashion business," River says meekly by way of explanation. "He's given me way too much. I think he thinks I'm cooler than I am."

"There's an entire section dedicated to gym wear," she says, hardly daring to believe it.

"We should focus on what's behind this second door. What's in here?" I ask.

"This is why I thought I might be able to help you collect the map and compass from the private collector's house," River begins, sounding apprehensive as he moves to my side. "My parents are in the technology business. They own a company that specializes in developing and producing new tech, and sometimes they'll … uh … let me keep some of the products they make."

"OK?" I say slowly.

"This room displays those things."

"What River is trying to say," Finn jumps in, sounding so happy he might burst, "is that he has an entire room of gadgets. Like, *spy gadgets*."

"I don't think they're technically marketed as spy gadgets," River comments.

"*Whoa*," Poppy says, hurrying over from the wardrobe. "This is awesome."

"Ella, behind glass display cabinets lining the room is every kind of state-of-the-art equipment you can imagine," Finn gushes. "Phones, watches, cameras, headsets, goggles, drones, trackers, electric scooters –" he pauses – "River, please tell me that is no ordinary umbrella on that stand over there."

"That is no ordinary umbrella," River confirms.

"Am I in heaven?" Finn breathes.

"You know, I thought that this whole heist idea was going to be a big failure," Poppy admits, before I hear her clap River on the back. "But now I think we might just pull it off."

CHAPTER TEN

The next morning, as planned, River calls to let me know that he and Irving have arrived at my house to pick up me, Maisie, Poppy and Finn to drive to Lord Jenson Almond's mansion in Surrey, just outside of London. According to Google, Lord Almond took over his dad's finance company at the age of thirty-three, but, having studied Greek mythology at Oxford University, has devoted a large portion of his life to expanding his impressive collection of priceless mythological artefacts. He is the owner of Hermes's compass and map – not that he knows it – and we're currently on the way to his mansion in one of the many big flashy cars belonging to River's mum and driven by Irving.

"And listen to this," Poppy adds, reading out Lord

Almond's biography from her phone, sitting in the backseat of the car with Finn and River. "He famously had a big fight with Everett Croft! Apparently, they got into this huge bidding war over an ancient dagger that an expert believed belonged to some dude called Peleus—"

"Hey, he was not 'some dude'," Finn corrects. "He was the father of Achilles."

"Not now, Finn," Poppy scolds. "Whoever he was, he had some dagger. These two rich men thought someone had dug it up and they both wanted it. Guess who won?"

"Since we're about to try to steal something from Lord Almond, I hope it's Everett Croft who has the dagger," Finn says.

"You're in luck, Finn, it *was* Everett Croft who bid the highest. Everett taunted Lord Almond in the press, calling him a 'loser'. But –" she lowers her voice dramatically – "then scandal hit."

"What happened?" I ask, drawn into the story.

"Turned out the dagger wasn't real. It was a big fake. So, obviously, Lord Almond couldn't have been happier and publicly called Everett Croft an 'idiot'."

"I would not want to be the expert who said that the dagger belonged to Peleus," I say.

"Me neither," River agrees.

"Poor guy never worked again," Poppy informs us. "Everett Croft made sure of it."

Irving announces, "We're almost at the desired location," from the driver's seat and I automatically sit up straight in the front seat, my calves pressed against Maisie's fur as she lies under my legs in the footwell. Irving made sure that the seat was pulled back enough for us to fit comfortably. River had to tell Irving a vague idea of what we were up to today, just so we could talk openly about it in front of him. Apparently, he listened to River's revelation this morning before they left to pick us up and his response was, "Very good, sir. What would you like for dinner this evening?"

It turns out that having a butler can be advantageous, especially one who doesn't ask any questions and helps you on secret missions to steal priceless artefacts and save the world.

"OK, don't park near the gate," River directs him. "Find a spot out of sight from the house somewhere here. We can walk the rest of the way."

"Very well," Irving replies.

"Is everyone clear about what they're doing?" River asks.

"Yes, we've been through it maybe five hundred times," Poppy says drily.

"Sorry, I'm a bit excited," River admits. "I've never been on a heist before."

The car slows and turns, pulling on to a bumpier surface before it comes to a stop.

"Perfect, the woodland surrounding the estate is hiding us nicely," River comments, and I hear him unzip the bag he's brought with him full of gadgets. The car door next to him opens, followed by the sound of him rummaging about in the bag, before he goes, "Aha! OK, let's get this up and running. I'll put my headset on."

"You need to wear a headset to fly a drone?" Poppy says, surprised.

"It's a VR headset so when I put it on, it gives me the view of the camera like I'm in it myself. It means I can pilot it from down here much easier," River explains.

There's a series of beeps and then the distinctive whir of a drone taking off.

"Remember not to fly too close to the house," Finn says nervously. "We don't want the security to notice it and be on high alert."

"Don't worry, Finn, I'll keep my distance," he

promises, as the sound of the drone grows distant, flying higher and higher into the sky.

"Can you see anything?" Poppy asks as we wait in anticipation for his report.

"There's a security guard in a booth just inside the gate. The driveway is short and it runs round the house to the back where there are six sports cars parked by the lawn which leads down to a big lake. Whoa, that's a nice Ferrari! I wonder which model it is."

"Focus, River," I remind him.

"Oh yeah, sorry. OK, there's another security guard chilling at the front of the house – he looks bored. He's swatting away a fly. He almost got it that time! Come on, mate, you can do it … *oooh*, missed him again!"

"*River*," Poppy prompts, while I fight a smile.

"Sorry! Hang on, I'll circle above the house." He falls quiet for a few moments and then says, "There's one light on upstairs, but no other lights on in the house that I can see. And there's security cameras on the outside, so I think we can take a guess that there will be more inside the house. Right, let me bring the drone home."

I slump back in my seat. "There will be more than

two people on his security team. There's got to be more men inside the house."

"Plus, a load of cameras everywhere. We don't even know where he keeps the map and compass," Poppy says dismally.

Irving coughs pointedly as the drone comes back in to land.

"Excuse the interruption, sir—"

"Please don't call me 'sir'!"

"I beg your pardon, *River*, but I wonder whether it might be worth taking the Off-Grid 240 when you go for your ... ahem ... country stroll with your friends."

River gasps. "Yes, good thinking, Irving!"

"What's the Off-Grid 240?" Finn asks in wonder.

"It's a device that my parents started developing, but they didn't get it perfect enough to bring to market," River explains, rummaging through his bag again. "Here it is."

"That's a Pokémon card," Finn states.

Poppy sniggers. "Vintage."

"You're *supposed* to think it's a Pokémon card," River says, unfazed. "It's designed to stick to a central control panel and shut it down for ten minutes. It would turn off door sensors, motion detectors, cameras and alarms."

"Are you *serious*?" Finn whispers.

"Cool, right?" River laughs. "The only problem is, it's a bit temperamental."

I grimace. "How temperamental?"

"During tests, it would sometimes only shut down a system for one or two minutes before it malfunctioned. But even that would be helpful, right?"

"It's a good distraction at least. I say we bring the Pokémon card," Poppy declares.

"Now we have an idea of the security, let's go through the plan again," Finn insists. "Ella, you and—"

"Maisie act as the distraction to get everyone through the gate," I finish for him.

"Once she's done that and we're through, *I* cause a distraction to lure the security guard away from the front door to give River and Finn the chance of getting into the house."

"And that's when Maisie and I will follow in, too," I state.

"When I'm in the house, I find the control panel and turn off the security," River says, a new addition to the plan thanks to Irving. "That will *hopefully* give us all more time to…"

"Find the room where Lord Almond keeps the map and compass," Finn jumps in, "which I'll be trying to locate thanks to these unbelievably awesome spy goggles that see through walls." He exhales. "I can't believe I said that and it's real life!"

"When Finn finds the items, we crack into the safe or wherever Lord Almond is keeping them using –" River pauses to rummage in his bag again before he finds what he's searching for – "*this*. A codebreaker that looks like a watch but can crack the code of most traditional safes."

Irving clears his throat again.

"May I also recommend that you bring your ballpoint pen, River?" he suggests breezily. "One never knows when one might feel a wave of inspiration to write."

Finn gasps. "Is it an *exploding* pen?"

"No, it's a lockpick," River says, and I can hear him smiling. "Do you think my parents would give me a pen that explodes?"

"That would be a bit out there," Finn admits, disappointed.

"Once we have the map and compass, we get out of there and hope no one catches us," I conclude.

"Good plan, let's go," Poppy says, clapping her hands together.

"Are you sure we're ready?" River asks, panicking at Poppy's hastiness. "It's not much of an escape plan."

"We don't have time to think about it," I say, reaching down to stroke Maisie's head. "And anyway, thanks to you, River, we're a lot more prepared than we would have been."

"Yeah, thank you for letting us borrow all these cool gadgets," Finn adds.

"I'm pleased to help," River says modestly. "I've never had the chance to show the gadgets to anyone, let alone use them. They didn't seem that exciting sitting in my room all this time gathering dust."

"What, none of your friends from your old school wanted to come check them out?" Finn asks, and I can hear him moving things around in River's bag as he looks through it.

River hesitates. "Uh … no. You're the only friends who have come to my house. Ever."

Finn stops what he's doing. The car falls silent. My stomach drops.

"Anyway, it's nice to share them with you," River adds quickly. "You should get going, Ella. We don't want to be here too long or too late."

"Yeah, you're right." I take a deep breath. "Everyone ready?"

"I guess so," Finn says nervously, as Irving opens his door to get out and hurry round to mine. "We'll be fine, right, Ella?"

"Yeah, we'll be fine," I say, climbing out of the car with Maisie and taking a deep breath. "Sometimes the hardest bit is putting one foot in front of the other."

And before I lose my nerve, I give Maisie her instruction and we set off together.

CHAPTER ELEVEN

"Can I help you?" The security guard asks as Maisie and I near Lord Almond's countryside mansion. I hear his footsteps approach the other side of the gate.

I place a hand on my heart and heave a dramatic sigh of relief, picking up the pace in the direction of his voice and breaking into a wide smile.

"Thank goodness! I've found someone!" I cry as Maisie comes to a stop at the gate, putting my all into a performance that plays into the stereotype that blind people walking on their own are lost. "I've been walking for ages and there's been no one to help."

"I'm not surprised, there's not much around here. Are you lost?"

I nod vigorously. "Completely! I'm visiting my

aunt in the village here, but I think my guide dog may have taken the wrong turning when we got off the bus."

"I'd say so. You're nowhere near the local village, I'm afraid."

"Oh no!"

"I'm sure it's not your dog's fault, though," he says, and I hear a welcome note of warmth in his voice. "It can be confusing finding your way around these parts. It's remote out here. I've got lost a few times myself. She's a lovely girl, your dog."

"You're a dog person?" I ask, brightening.

"*Am I?*" he gushes. "I grew up with three goldies. Your one reminds me of our second one, Belle. My sister named her that because she was so beautiful. The same shiny golden hair as your dog, and the same bright eyes. Oh look –" he chuckles as I hear Maisie begin to pant a little – "she's smiling at me. Golden retrievers have the best grin."

"I can take her harness off and you can pet her if you like," I offer.

He gasps hopefully. "Really? If you're sure you're happy for her to have a break."

"She'd love that, she's big on cuddles."

"All mine were, too," he says fondly. "Hang on,

stay where you are, let me open this gate. What's your dog's name?"

"Maisie. And I'm Ella."

"Well, Maisie and Ella, I'm Dennis and it's an honour to meet you. Technically I'm working, too, but I'd say there's no harm in the two of us having a quick break."

He retreats and a moment later there's a loud buzzing sound and the creak of the gate automatically swinging open.

"Forward," I instruct Maisie, and we go on through, stopping at the booth.

Bending down to remove her harness, I manoeuvre our position so that Maisie is turned to face the gate, the mansion behind us. Her collar jingles as she shakes, her tail wagging in excitement as her new friend comes to make a big fuss of her. My careful positioning has worked; he crouches down to face her, which leaves his back to the gate.

Hopefully, he won't notice anyone creeping in through the open gates behind him.

"Hello, you," Dennis greets Maisie warmly. "You're a lovely girl. Such soft fur! Did you get a little lost? It happens to us all, my girl, don't you worry. I'll help you and your owner find where you need to be."

I hear the slobbery sound of Maisie licking his face and he bursts out laughing.

"That's a nice 'thank you'! It's like you can understand what I'm saying."

"I always think that," I tell him. "People say dogs don't speak our language, but I'm convinced Maisie speaks mine. My sister teases me for talking to her."

"No one understands you like a dog does. Goldies are very clever, too. You know, Belle used to be able to do loads of tricks."

"That's amazing!"

"And she wasn't allowed upstairs, but she'd wait until my parents had gone to sleep, then she'd sneak to my room, push the door open and jump up to curl into bed with me." He chortles happily at the memory. "I miss that dog. I miss *all* those dogs."

"Do you have one now?"

"Nah, I can't, not with my work. This security gig is long hours. Do you know whose house this is? Lord Almond's." He puts on a baby voice to speak directly to Maisie again. "And he doesn't approve of us taking time off, does he Miss Maisie? No, he doesn't. I bet you love your job, though, don't you? Yes, you do, you clever, clever girl. Such a *good girly-girly-goo-goo*. You are the *best girl*, aren't you, I can tell. Yes, you are, clever *Maisie-moo-moo*."

While I'm fighting my urge to giggle, Maisie laps up the attention. Her tail is wagging fiercely against my leg and I hear her lick him all over his face again. Dennis sighs.

"Sorry, Maisie, I should probably get back to work," he says regretfully, groaning as he straightens and I hear him wiping the dirt off his trousers. "Now, where exactly is your aunt's address? I can try to—"

Right on cue, a car alarm rings through the air. Then another one. And another one.

It sounds like Poppy worked out a good distraction.

"I should go check that out. You and Maisie wait here, I'll be back in a moment," Dennis instructs.

"All right, thank you!" I call out as I hear him hurry off down the drive.

Quickly putting Maisie's harness back on, I wait a minute or so, and with the alarms still sounding, I say to her, "Find the way, Maisie, find the way."

She knows I'm asking her to use her initiative and sets off at once in the direction of the house. My heart is hammering as we approach the house, terrified at being caught. When the alarms stop ringing, I bite my lip nervously, knowing the guards might return back to their posts at any moment. But then I hear someone bellow from the other side of the house, "The Ferrari! Oh my god, it's headed for the lake!"

And someone else yells back, "Quick! Try to stop it! It's rolling down the hill!"

Maisie stops, alerting me to the steps leading up to the front door, and I freeze when I hear hurried footsteps coming towards me from round the side of the house.

"Ella, it's me," Poppy says. "Quick, let's go in. Finn and River are already in there. Don't worry, I think I got the security team out of the house. They should be busy for a while." She gasps as we step through the front door. "Whoa, this house is huge! And so *regal*. Chandeliers, marble floor, giant oil paintings, red carpet up the stairs. It looks like the set of a period drama! I feel like I should be wearing a bonnet or a tiara or something."

"What exactly did you do out there?" I ask curiously.

"I tried to pick the locks of the sports cars and set off the alarms," she informs me in a low, mischievous voice. "The Ferrari was open, though, so I took off the handbrake, popped it into first gear and … gave it a nudge."

"You gave the Ferrari a nudge?" I repeat in a nervous whisper.

"The lawn is on a downward slope towards the lake."

"Poppy! We just needed a distraction! You're not meant to drown his car collection!"

"It's only *one* of them," she says breezily. "And anyway, the security team will have got there in time before it reached the water." She hesitates. "Maybe."

We're distracted by a loud *thump* followed by a fit of coughs from across the hallway, making both of us jump. I grip Poppy's arm nervously, but she pats my hand.

"It's only Finn. He's walked into the old curtains at the back of the room and I think may have inhaled a cloud of centuries-old dust," she whispers, amused, before there's another *bump*. "And now he's turned round and walked straight into a door." She raises her voice to a loud hiss: "Finn! What are you *doing*?"

"It's these spy goggles!" he replies in a frustrated, hushed tone. "River said they can see through walls, but I can't see a thing!"

"That's because you haven't turned them on," River says, entering the room. I hear him stride over the floor in Finn's direction before there's a short, sharp beep. "There you go."

"Oh *wow*! Yeah, that's *much* better!" Finn says, and I hear Poppy facepalm.

"Great work, everyone. The security team are all outside," River tells us. "I found the control room and fixed the Off-Grid 240 to the panel. For now, the alarm system is down."

"For how long?" I ask.

"Could be fifteen minutes, could be two. We need to work fast. Finn, can you tell us if it looks like there are any artefacts on this floor?"

"Nope, I don't think so," Finn says, as he paces back and forth across the hallway. "There's no items on display, or safes in any of the walls on this floor that I can see."

"Let's go upstairs, then," Poppy directs, taking the lead.

Maisie and I follow her, with Finn next to us and River behind. When we get to the landing, Finn takes a moment to examine his surroundings.

"The door at the end of the corridor to our left," he says excitedly. "It's full of glass cases displaying artefacts! Like a mini museum."

"That must be his collection," I say, hope zipping through me. "Can you see one that holds what looks like a piece of old parchment with a paper weight?"

"Yes! It's right in the middle."

"Quick, let's go," Poppy says, and I hear her pelt down towards it, jiggling the door handle. "It's locked! Finn, use your exploding pen."

"Again, it doesn't explode," he clarifies, going to join her as Maisie and I wait with Finn. "It picks locks."

"Whatever, just get us in!" Poppy instructs.

"It's not working," River reveals in exasperation after a series of clicking sounds.

"Finn, where's the door of the room next to it?" I ask him urgently.

"The second one to your left. But why?" he asks, confused.

Taking Maisie to that door, I try the handle and it swings open. "Is there a way through to the collection from this room?"

"No," Poppy answers, appearing at my side. "But there's a window."

"How does that help?" River asks, as Poppy marches into the room.

There's a sliding sound of a window being opened before I'm hit by a gentle breeze.

"I can climb through, hop over to the next ledge along, climb in through that window and then open the door from the other side to let you lot in," Poppy answers casually.

"*Hop over to the next ledge*?" Finn repeats in horror.

"Poppy, no! It's too dangerous!" I tell her.

"We need to get in that room, right?" she says, as I hear her heave herself up on to the windowsill.

"Yes, but—"

"We've come this far and we're running out of time, right?"

"Poppy—"

"Nothing important is ever easy. See? I do listen to you sometimes, Ella."

"When I said that, I didn't mean *go window hopping*!"

Her chuckle is muffled by the breeze. She must be through the window now, gripping on to the outside of it as she shuffles along the ledge.

"It's not like we've never done anything dangerous before," I hear her respond.

"River, please go outside to watch her from there!" I beg him.

"It's too late, she's already reaching across and stretching her foot over to the other ledge along," he whispers in response, gripping my forearm.

131

"And she's … done it! She's made it to the next window!"

"I can't watch," Finn whimpers.

River leaves my side to scurry over to the window to report on her progress as my stomach churns with nerves. "OK, she's carefully trying to get the window open. I think it's a bit stiff, it's old." He gasps and my heart lurches. "She's opened it! And … and she's swung herself in the room! She did it, she did it!"

We make our way back to the end of the landing just in time to hear the satisfactory clunk of a bolt sliding and the door swinging open.

"I should totally audition for the next *Mission Impossible*," Poppy declares, catching her breath. "I'm wasted at school."

"You should know, I'm cross at you for doing that," I say, grabbing her hand and squeezing it. "But also grateful. Thank you."

"Here it is," River calls over, having weaved his way through the glass cabinets to the centre of the room. "I'll see if the lockpicker works on this case."

There's a beat of silence and then … *click*.

"It worked," River whispers in disbelief.

Poppy inhales sharply, squeezing my hand even tighter. Within moments, River is back with us, his voice shaky as he says, "Here, Poppy. Take a look at this."

The Eye of Horus immediately starts to grow warm against my skin.

"Ella," Finn gasps in amazement, "it was blank before, but something is happening. Black ink is appearing across the map. I'm not sure what it means, but it's—"

Suddenly, a whirring sound interrupts him, like a machine being switched back on.

"Oh no," River groans. "The cameras are working, I can see the red lights blinking in the corners of the room!"

"Are these red lines across the room … *lasers*?" Poppy asks nervously.

"You mean the ones we're all standing in? Yep. They're sensor lasers," River answers in a defeated tone. "Three, two, one…"

A loud alarm pierces the air.

"Our time is up," River says. "We need to get out of here before we're caught!"

"Too late for that, I'm afraid," comes an unfamiliar man's voice from the doorway behind me.

"Wh-who are you?" Finn stammers.

"I'm Lord Jenson Almond and you're currently

standing in my home, holding my things," he says in an eerily calm tone. "Which begs the question, who exactly are *you*?"

CHAPTER TWELVE

No one answers. Lord Almond sighs with disappointment.

"A quiet bunch of thieves," he remarks, before clicking his fingers with a loud snap, making me jump. "Take the parchment from *her*, and the gold weight from *him* and bring all of them downstairs."

I realize quickly that he must be talking to his security team as I hear River try to keep hold of the compass before it's wrenched from his grip by someone else. Lord Almond's footsteps grow distant down the landing as he heads downstairs and we're all escorted down behind him.

"I thought we were friends, Maisie," Dennis grumbles.

He sounds genuinely disappointed and my heart

sinks with guilt. It doesn't seem right to have deceived a dog person, especially one who is such a huge fan of golden retrievers.

Once we've gathered downstairs in the hallway, Lord Almond clears his throat.

"So," he begins, "before I call the police and have you arrested, would you care to give me an explanation as to why you'd go to such lengths to steal something like this? You all seem a bit ... young to be so interested in a bit of old parchment. You could have taken anything – priceless art, precious jewellery, antique weapons. Seems odd that you'd ignore all those and go straight for, well, *these*."

"I'm sorry that we broke into your house," I begin earnestly. "But we need those items, and we didn't think we had the time to try to persuade you to hand them over if we asked."

He snorts. "Of course I wouldn't *hand* them over. Do you have any idea what these are and how much they're worth?"

"Do *you*?"

There's a beat of silence. He's clearly shocked by my response.

"I ... well, yes, they're priceless," he says uneasily. "While scholars are not entirely sure what they are, they have been able to provide me with enough information to guarantee their value and antiquity – such items would have belonged to a being that was worshipped and revered." He pauses. "What do you think you know about them?"

"I know that what you're holding in your hands could save the world."

More silence. But this time it's broken by his cackle of laughter, followed by loyal sniggers and chortles from his henchmen.

"Save the world from what exactly?" he asks eventually through wheezes.

"The unbearable noise that keeps happening. It's going to grow out of control, sparking waves of rage and fury until real battle noise is the only way to drown it out."

"I'm sorry, I don't think I caught your name," he prompts, highly amused.

"My name is Ella Jones," I say, lifting my chin.

"And that's Maisie, her guide dog," Dennis informs him. "Now, I don't want to speak for Maisie, Lord Almond, but I don't think any of this was her idea."

"Yes, thank you, Dennis," Lord Almond says drily. "Obviously I didn't suspect the golden retriever to be the brains of the operation."

"They are a very intelligent breed," Dennis mutters defensively.

"Well, Ella Jones," Lord Almond continues, ignoring Dennis, "I'm not exactly sure how you think a sheet of parchment and what might be some kind of gold astrological device is going to save the world from the noise, but I admit I'm curious to find out. Would you enlighten me?"

"It's not an astrological device, it's a compass, and that's not a sheet of parchment, it's a map," Finn tells him pompously.

"A rather poor map, considering it's blank," Lord Almond sneers.

"We don't have the time to explain it to you. Please believe me," I plead, knowing that it's a longshot. "If you want the noise to stop, you have to let us borrow those items."

"I'm going to need more than the word of a little girl before I let you wander out of my house in possession of some artefacts that not only cost a lot of money but are of great historical and archaeological importance. Not to mention the mythological connotations."

"She can show you," River says suddenly. "Let her hold them."

"*Excuse* me?"

"If you let her hold the map, then it will show the way," River explains, and I hear him take a confident step forward to stand next to me. "Ella is the one who's meant to have it. That's what Ailynn said. She's worthy of it, so it will work for her."

I'm distracted by my pendant growing hot, my hand flying up to it.

"Oh no," I whisper.

"Who on Earth is *Ailynn*?" Lord Almond asks quizzically. "You know, I'm tired of this. You're all breaking and entering. It's time I called the police. Dennis, please could you…"

He trails off.

We all hear it coming. Like always, it starts as a threatening faint hum in the background, like a train in the distance rumbling towards you with no signs of stopping.

"No," Lord Almond says, swallowing audibly. "No, no, no, not again!"

"Everyone listen to me," I say desperately, raising my voice as the noise grows louder and louder. "Fight as much as you can against this! You are stronger than the anger it makes you feel! Try not to let the rage take over you, listen for my voice through this noise. I promise you that you will be OK. Everything is going to be all right!"

But it's no use. The noise becomes deafening, swallowing my voice, and Lord Almond and his security team begin to yell and cry out for it to stop. I reach for Poppy's arm and hold it, but I don't know where Finn and River are, both having retreated to a wall somewhere in the room, cowering from the noise they can't possibly escape.

And someone in the distance begins to laugh.

"Poppy, can you hear me?" I ask desperately, grabbing both her wrists.

"Ella! Ella, yes, I … I think I … are you there?" she says through sobs.

"I'm here! I'm right here."

"The noise is fading, but everyone else is still suffering from it," she tells me, as Lord Almond's security team begin to shout, blaming each other for this situation, angrily accusing other members of their team for letting a bunch of kids into the house. "How is this happening, Ella? As soon as you touched me, it went away!"

"It's the Eye of Horus, it's protecting you. Can you hear someone laughing?"

"What?" she says before dismissing my question,

141

too distracted to focus. "Ella, you were right. You were right all along. I—"

She yelps as something crashes behind me.

"What was that?" I ask her, placing a protective hand on Maisie's head, who is standing by me whining, worried about everyone's behaviour.

"One of the guards has picked up the vase of flowers that was on the table by the staircase and thrown it at his colleague!" she tells me. "He ducked, but now he's trying to rip off part of the banister railing to retaliate!"

"Is that Finn and River shouting at each other?" I ask, horrified.

"Yes," Poppy replies, sounding equally astounded. "Finn is blaming River for us being caught and River is telling Finn that he doesn't deserve the spy goggles. Ella, it's getting worse."

"You mean the Eye of Horus isn't working for you?" I ask, panicking.

"No, it is. I mean, before you grabbed me, it felt like ... like I couldn't handle it. The anger bubbling up inside me. I *had* to scream. It's much worse than it was before." She grips me tightly. "What are we going to do? We have to get that map!"

"First, help me over to Finn and River so the Eye of Horus can help them, too."

Before she can do as I ask, the noise stops. Sighs of relief ripple through the room before the bitter accusations and anger creep back into play.

"You threw that vase at me," someone growls. "You could have hurt me!"

"What about you swinging that banister railing like a baseball bat? You always like to blame everyone else for your actions. This is why I don't like working with you," his companion replies crossly.

"Well guess what? I don't like working with you!"

"Both of you be quiet!" Lord Almond snaps.

"Why should we?" the banister-wielder responds defensively.

"Yeah, why should we?" the vase-hurler echoes. "You do nothing but boss us around! I'm tired of it! You get your own car out of the lake!"

"It's your fault that my car is in the lake in the first place! What's the point in having security if a child can come in and take what she likes? You're all useless!"

"Stop it! All of you stop it!" I cry out. "This is what he wants."

The room falls silent.

"What who wants?" Lord Almond demands to know.

"Someone who is determined to throw the world into chaos by using noise to spur rage," I explain, throwing my hand up in exasperation. "It's working. Can't you hear yourselves? He's winning. Do you like feeling this way? Angry and resentful?"

"No," Lord Almond mutters. "I must admit that I don't."

"Then please, let me borrow the map and the compass. Let me do something to try to stop this before it's too late. I understand why you'd be reluctant to believe me, but…"

I trail off as it dawns on me just how ridiculous this all must seem to someone like Lord Almond. A twelve-year-old girl and her friends demanding he hand over his priceless artefacts so that they can protect humankind from chaos. It's not lost on me how strange it is that it should be me who is in this position. How has it come to be that I am the one entrusted with the fate of the world? I never asked for this and, while I may act as though I'm confident in what I have to do, that doesn't mean I don't have moments where I doubt myself. Moments where I wonder whether I can do this. Or whether I'll lose.

But no matter the outcome, I have to try. That's why I keep going.

I hold out my hand in the direction of Lord Almond's voice. "If you let me hold the map for a second, you'll see that we're telling the truth. If nothing happens, you can take it back from me. *Please*."

He takes a moment to consider my request and then reluctantly says, "All right. It sounds absurd. I think it's a government conspiracy myself, but if you've gone to all this trouble to break in because you think that this piece of parchment has anything to do with it, well –" he presses the map into the palm of my outstretched hand – "it's worth a try."

My fingers tremble as I carefully unfold the thick parchment. Having gone cold since the noise stopped, the Eye of Horus grows hot again. I exhale in relief. It feels like hope.

"*It can't be*," Lord Almond breathes. "It was blank before! But … the lines … there are black ink lines appearing!"

"Told you," River says, returning to stand at my shoulder.

I hear the others gather round me, gasping in chorus as they witness the impossible. I give a small smile. "It's the Map of Movement."

"Here, Ella, bring it over to this table," Finn

suggests over by the staircase. "It's empty now that the vase of flowers isn't here. You can rest it on top."

"See? I was helpful," mutters the security guard who threw the vase.

Moving there flanked by my audience, I lay out the map and run my hands across it.

The lines are raised and they continue to move into position.

"It's a moving tactile map," I say as my smile widens. "It's amazing."

"It's incredible," Finn adds, placing a hand on my shoulder.

"It's magical," Poppy remarks.

"Am I dreaming?" Lord Almond asks, before I hear him pat himself down. "No, I'm not in my silk pyjamas. This is happening. This is really *happening*. All this time, I had no idea what it was – it's a *map*. A moving map! How is this possible?"

"It's a map created by a trickster god, remember Ella," River warns quietly. "Ailynn told us that Hermes would make things personal to its reader."

"He's doing just that," I inform him. "The lines are transforming into Braille."

"What does it say?" Poppy asks. "Can you read it out for us?"

I run my fingers along the series of raised dots before reading it out loud:

> *"A brave young girl with too much to lose,*
> *Begin this journey if you so choose.*
> *Round your neck, the protective eye,*
> *But will you be saved from the god*
>   *you defy?*
>
> *A worthy seeker, but the path is wrought,*
> *with dangers in which you will be caught.*
> *The shield reveals the tests in store,*
> *Destiny entwined with art and folklore.*
>
> *First, a pursuit with those you hold dear,*
> *But then comes confusion, panic and fear.*
> *But more is due to lie in wait,*
> *for it is then that you shall meet your Fate."*

The Braille vanishes. Then one last question rises up in the parchment. I cut through the silence that's fallen since I finished the poem to read it out, my voice hoarse:

> *"Do you wish to continue?"*

I lift my hand off the paper. My heart is thumping against my chest loudly, and I wonder if everyone can hear it.

"I-I've been thinking," Lord Almond stammers in a high-pitched voice, "you can have the map. And this thing, too." I hear him tap on the compass. "Yes, they're yours to borrow. Clearly, you might be on to something here and I'd hate to get in the way of your ... uh ... destiny."

"Thanks. We'll get them right back to you," Poppy says drily.

"No rush, no rush!" he squeaks. "You do what you need to do."

"Pursuit, confusion, panic, fear and fate," Finn echoes from the poem in a low, serious voice. "All of those are depicted on the Shield of Hercules. It sounds like those will be the themes of the challenges you have to face to get it."

"Ella, are you sure you should do this?" Poppy asks nervously.

Nodding, I run my fingers over the question still waiting for me to answer:

"Do you wish to continue?"

"Yes," I say, the Eye of Horus growing hot. "I'm ready."

The Braille question vanishes and another poem appears:

> "Now in Pursuit of a treasure most dear,
> You've accepted to face all that you fear.
> Let us go to a place that for you left a scar,
> This journey will show you just who
>   you are."

CHAPTER THIRTEEN

Finn puts his arm round my shoulders.

"Wherever it takes you, you won't be alone. We're coming too," he says.

I shake my head. "No. This map is going to be personal to me. The challenges that I come up against on the way will be personal, too. Only I need to face and overcome them – no one else. I'm not going to put you through it all when you don't need to."

"You don't have a say in the matter," Poppy declares. "Finn's right, we're coming."

"But—"

"You might need us, Ella," Finn insists. "The best way to overcome personal challenges is to share them, don't you think? We're not letting you do this on your own."

"We might be able to help," Poppy says.

"We've come this far together," River adds. "You're not getting rid of us now, not when it's just starting to get interesting."

Maisie barks twice and then snorts.

"There you go. Maisie's in too," Poppy says. "You're stuck with us, Ella. Whatever journey you're about to go on, you've got company."

"Thank you," I croak, fighting back grateful tears.

River gasps. "Hey, the lines are back on the map and they're moving!"

I run my hands over the map and find that River is right, the Braille has been replaced by raised lines that are twisting and joining together, forming some kind of illustration.

"It looks like the outline of a country," Finn says in wonder.

"That's because it is," I tell him, tracing the outline with my fingers. "It's Scotland and the islands surrounding it. The Scotland outline is fading away, though."

"That's right. The only outline left behind is a cluster of islands to the west of Scotland," Finn observes. "Are those the Outer Hebrides?"

"Yes," I say, as more outlines disappear, the

northernmost islands of the Outer Hebrides dropping away until there's only the southernmost islands left.

I know where it's taking me before the map finishes its work. Sure enough, everything fades until only one island remains of the Outer Hebrides on the map.

Its outline stands alone beneath my fingertips.

"Where is that?" River asks.

"I believe that's Barra," Lord Almond reveals from behind us. He must be peering over our shoulders. "A small, beautiful island in the Outer Hebrides of Scotland. I've been there before. The beaches are stunning: soft-white sand, crystal-blue sea. The plane lands on the beach, you know. And the seafood is absolutely exquisite. You must order the lobster."

Poppy snorts. "I'm not sure we'll have much time to sit and order lobster. Ella, why would the map take us to Barra?"

"Have you been there before?" River asks.

"Yes, on a family holiday a few years ago," Poppy tells him. "It was Dad's idea to go there, I think. It was a fun trip. At least –" she hesitates – "I thought it was."

"Ailynn said that Hermes's map takes you to the place you feared the most," River notes. He hesitates and then asks gently, "Ella, does it make sense that the map is taking you to Barra?"

I'm finding it hard to speak. My stomach is twisting itself into knots, a lump is building in my throat and tears are threatening to spill over at any moment. The moment I realized where I was going, I was hit by a flood of unwelcome memories.

I can't answer River with words. So, I give a small, sharp nod.

Clearly noticing that I need a moment to collect myself, Finn steps back and announces, "Right, looks like we're going to Scotland. Lord Almond, thanks for lending us these items. We'll take good care of them."

"I wish you the best of luck with your journey and I hope, for the sake of the world, you succeed," Lord Almond declares solemnly, like a king sending his knights off to battle.

"I'll give Irving a call and get him to bring the car round," River says.

"Then we need to work out how we're going to get to Scotland," Poppy points out. "It will be long and expensive. How are we going to pay for it?"

"That won't be a problem," River tells her. "I can cover the tickets. For all of us."

"*What?*" she says in surprise.

"I'll pay for the journey. Irving can help us organize it. We can leave straight away."

"That's super generous of you, River, are you sure?" Finn checks.

"Honestly, if there's anything I'd want to spend my money on, it would be this."

"What, on a random trip to a small Scottish island?" Poppy says, unconvinced.

"On a trip with friends," he corrects.

We fall into silence as he walks away to give his butler a call.

To get to Barra we need to catch the sleeper train from London to Glasgow, and then a flight from there to the island itself first thing in the morning. River kept to his promise, deciding the quickest route with Irving's help and buying the train tickets. We've promised to pay him back, but he says he doesn't want us to. He says it's exciting for him to be a part of this adventure. I don't have the heart to tell him that once he's on the adventure, he might not find it exciting at all.

It's much more likely he'll be afraid.

But his excitement, combined with the bravery and selflessness of Poppy and Finn, is helping me to keep going when I'm scared of what I've got us all into. If it were only Maisie and I, it would be worrying enough, but the fact that my sister and friends are going to face these challenges with me is even more terrifying. I wish they weren't here so they were safe and protected, but at the same time, I don't think I could do this without them.

The train to Glasgow isn't busy. Since the bouts of unbearable noise keep happening more often and without any warning, a lot of people have made the decision to stay at home where they know they can't hurt themselves or anyone else. There are reports that the government is going to announce that everyone should stay home as official advice, although that hasn't happened yet. I've been worrying about Mum and Dad, but Poppy has told me that she's got it under control. Mum's working extra shifts at the hospital, and Poppy has phoned Dad to tell him that we're with River. Insisting on accompanying us on the journey, Irving was able to speak to him on the phone and confirm that we're safe and well looked after. I think Dad assumed Irving was River's dad, and when Poppy said we were "with River for the weekend", he took that to mean we were at River's house for a sleepover.

"Technically, we're not lying to him," Poppy told me after we hung up the phone. "We're just not telling him the whole truth. It's totally fine."

I was sceptical, but I didn't have a choice.

Thanks to the lack of crowds at the train station, finding our platform and carriage was smooth, and we got seats no problem. I usually make my way towards a train filled with anxiety, convinced that *something* is going to be a problem. I never know what it will be, but for someone like me, the act of getting on a train is never easy. The carriage will be crowded, which makes it hard for Maisie to get me to my seat; assistance workers won't necessarily turn up when I book them, so I have to navigate the station and platform without any help; ticket machines will be out of order and announcements about changes to the service won't be clear; or there will be obstacles or lifts that don't work, which means Maisie and I have to unexpectedly use escalators, which is extra-stressful as Maisie hasn't been formally trained to use them yet. It was like that before the Day of Darkness and it's still like that now.

But thankfully, with my sister and friends and a near-empty train, we board it without any issues and soon the others are all in their cabins, dozing as the train rattles out of the city and through the countryside towards Scotland. I didn't want to go to bed just yet. I'm too distracted by worries about the journey ahead. The compass is safely stowed in my bag and the map is in my pocket. Maisie is lying under my legs. Irving stayed up with me for a while, but retreated to his cabin when he realized I wanted to be on my own. Left alone with my thoughts, I stroke Maisie's head for comfort as I think about returning to Barra.

Hermes is right to take me there. I thought I'd never go back.

The last time I was there was before I lost my sight. I had been for a routine eye check with Poppy. I remember so clearly the ophthalmologist's expression when she told my mum that I needed to go to the hospital. Her forehead was creased with worry, her mouth a hard, straight line. Mum took me there immediately and that was when I was diagnosed with a rare genetic condition. I was told I would lose my sight. It's a strange feeling when someone tells you something like that. This is *going* to happen. Nothing we can do.

It felt crushing, but also surreal. I heard what they were saying, but it was like my brain couldn't quite believe it. That week, Dad booked a long weekend in Barra. My parents thought it was a good time to go away as a family, escape to somewhere beautiful, quiet and peaceful. Barra is the perfect place for that. It feels separate to the world.

"There's something about this place," Mum said as we stood on the beach and she looked out at the blue water that was sparkling in the sunshine. "There's a magical spirit to Barra, don't you think?"

We all agreed with her. One evening, we took our time wandering up to the top of the hills to look out at the spectacular view. Miles and miles of countryside covered in colourful wildflowers and long green grass stretched out before us, the water glimmering in the distance, and the sun setting on the horizon casting the sky in a purple and deep-orange hue.

It's the sort of view that artists dream of painting. It was so beautiful that the whole family fell into silence when we reached the top. Not even Poppy said anything as we gazed out at it, the breeze whipping our hair around our faces, everyone but me smiling out at it.

A dread had crept in and gripped my heart.

It was squeezing it so tight, I felt like I couldn't breathe.

As I stood on the hills of Barra, I realized that a day would come when I would no longer be able to see a view like this one. I wouldn't be able to see anything at all.

I realized that I was going to lose who I was.

I remember running down the hill as fast as I could, Mum and Dad calling out after me. I tripped and fell over on my hands and knees. When they reached me, I wouldn't tell them what had triggered my panic, I couldn't bear to say it out loud, but I think they probably knew. Mum held me close and stroked my hair, and she cried with me. I tried to shake away the fear, but it gripped me for the whole trip. When we visited a medieval castle the next day and I got to the top before anyone else, I looked out over the sea and felt so angry I wanted to scream.

Why me? I shouted into the wind. *Why did this have to happen to me?*

That image of the mesmerizing Barra countryside is one that I tried desperately to remember for months after I lost my sight, gripping on to the thoughts over and over as the memory became fuzzier. The more I begged my mind to remember, the more it faded because I couldn't refresh the visual memory.

The train jerks, jolting me from my thoughts. I can

hear Poppy's gentle snores. I quickly use the back of my hand to wipe the stream of tears from my cheeks. I feel Maisie's cold, wet nose nudge my ankle. She can sense that something's not right, and she's trying to remind me that I'm not alone. Although that's always comforting, there's nothing she, or anyone else, can do to help what I'm feeling right now as we make our way to Barra once more. It's the same feeling I had as I stood on those cliffs and at the top of the castle.

True fear.

CHAPTER FOURTEEN

The train is nearing Glasgow the next morning when my pendant begins to grow warm and a feeling of unease washes through my body. We're all groggy from the short amount of sleep we managed to get. Finn, Poppy and I have just finished some breakfast that we bought from the trolly, and Irving is sitting at the table opposite us, his teacup clattering against the saucer as he places it down. River is making his way down the aisle towards the toilet. I clasp the Eye of Horus, terrified of what's about to happen.

And then it comes before I have a chance to warn the others, an irksome hum that quickly ascends into a chorus of screams and clashing metal. As the unbearable noise grows, the driver hits the brakes hard. The train begins to screech against the tracks as it slows abruptly. I lurch forward and then regain my balance, gripping on to my seat, while Maisie sits up and presses herself against my legs. I hold out my hands.

"Everyone put your hands on me!" I cry. "Just do as I say! Quickly, before the noise gets worse!"

With my pendant growing warm, I feel Finn and Poppy grip my arm just in time as the noise roars through the carriage. But Irving and River are too far to reach me. I hear River cry out in distress, while Irving bellows in fury. I desperately try to work out how to help them when they can't hear me above the din.

"I can still hear the noise, but it's not making me angry like before," Finn says. "It's horrible, but it's not hurting me!"

"Focus on your breathing and really listen," I advise him, trying to do the same myself. "The Eye of Horus will protect us."

I shudder as I hear River bang his fist against the seats.

"Can either of you reach him?" I ask.

"He's too far away, we'd have to let go of you," Poppy tells me. "I can try…"

"No, the moment you let go, the noise will overwhelm you. You won't be able to reach him, and you may not be able to hear my voice through it and get back to me."

I gasp as River cries out in torment.

"What are you doing, all sitting there calmly?" he screams at us, his words dripping in uncontrollable anger and resentment. "This is all your fault! You can make it stop, but you won't. You're keeping the antidote to yourself!"

"River, no! I want to help you," I reply, doing my best to stay collected although my stomach is twisting in anxious knots. "If you come this way, then—"

I'm interrupted as he yelps in pain, a reaction that causes Poppy to whimper in sympathy as her nails dig into my skin.

"He's fallen to the floor," Poppy tells me. "He's literally writhing in pain!"

"You won't help me, will you!" River bellows, his voice filling the carriage. "I will always be on the outside! I'll never be one of you! I can see that now."

"No, River, please, try to listen to me," I plead.

"This journey is doomed!" Irving shouts at the top of his lungs, making me jump. "What is the point? Why am I bothering helping a bunch of kids? There's nothing we can do. Nothing that will save us now! We're all *doomed*."

"He doesn't mean that," I tell Poppy and Finn urgently, as I can feel their hands trembling. "It's the noise, it's so excruciating and the only way to help the pain is for them to get angry at nothing, OK? Don't let what they're saying affect you."

"We know," Finn croaks. "But I'm not sure witnessing this pain is any more bearable than experiencing it myself."

I swallow, knowing exactly what Finn means. It's torturous to hear River and Irving like this and feel so helpless. And just when I think it can't get worse, I hear that laugh again. Deep and chilling – a vicious cackle underlying the noise and covering my skin in goosebumps. Somehow, I know it's for me, that laugh. As though he's watching us and he wants me to know that he could stop it if he wanted to, but he won't.

It's Homados laughing. I believe that now.

But if his presence is meant to scare me off, it has the opposite effect. He may terrify me, but that's even more reason to not let him win. I won't let fear of him stop me.

"Right, come on," I say to Finn and Poppy, "guide me towards Irving. Help me reach him."

"Don't you dare come near me," Irving spits. "Don't touch me!"

"Ignore him," I instruct, ready to get to my feet, tears in my eyes. "Come on, we can do this!"

The noise stops suddenly.

I slump back in my seat. Shaken, Poppy squeezes my arm while Finn is up on his feet, hurrying down the aisle to River. I hear him stumble backwards when River yells to leave him alone.

"It's OK, River, the noise has finished now. It's going to be OK," Finn says calmly.

"How do you know?" River snaps, the rage still yet to subside.

Finn doesn't have the answer to that. I can hear Irving's attempts to steady his breathing as he comes out of his rage, and then he says hoarsely, "River, it's OK, I'm coming to you," before I hear him slide out from his seat to join Finn and River down the aisle.

After a while, the train conductor's voice comes crackling through the intercom: "We have come to a stop just outside of a station, and after such a … horrifying event, we've decided to pull forward to the station and make an unscheduled stop there so that any passengers can alight who wish to do so. There will be a train on the platform opposite that will be returning to London in a few minutes. This service is still going on to Glasgow, but I should warn passengers that it looks unlikely many trains will run after today due to the … uh … irregular noise complaints."

As the train begins to move again, Poppy shifts in her seat. "Ella, are you sure you want to keep going? Are you sure this is what you want?"

I don't say anything, doubts creeping into my mind as I think about how relieved I'd feel to get on to the train back to London, forgetting the challenges Hermes promised. Someone else could fix it all. I could go home to Mum and Dad and stay safe with Poppy and Maisie. I wouldn't have to go back to Barra. I wouldn't have to face any fears.

Finn and Irving have managed to persuade River to sit back down with us again and I hear them slide into their seats.

"River," I say, reaching for him and finding his hand. His fingers are still trembling. "Are you OK? I'm so sorry I couldn't reach you to help you."

"I'm fine," he says in a voice that shows he's definitely not fine at all.

He pulls his hand free from mine.

The train slows and comes to a stop at the station. I hear the beep of the doors before they swish open. An announcement travels down the platform outside about a train due to depart for London.

"We have a chance to turn back," Poppy says.

I think of River a few minutes ago and how the noise turned him into someone I know he's not. That scares me more than any of my other fears. I won't let Homados turn the world into somewhere full of hate and battle. A world where everyone loses who they are.

I have to at least *try* to stop him.

"I won't turn back. I won't give up," I say.

The train doors shut, and we set off once more.

With the Eye of Horus still warm against my neck, I pull out the map and lay it out across the table. Knowing it has my attention, it springs to life.

"It's Braille," Poppy says, as I run my fingers across the sheet to find where the raised dots are appearing. "What is it saying this time, Ella?"

"It's another poem. It reads:

> *Remaining in Pursuit, you held firm*
> *and fast,*
> *No turning back, the first test is passed.*
> *Not for glory or wealth, for power or*
> *throne,*
> *You stayed the course for others alone.*

> *A worthy contender you may still prove,*
> *Yet beware young hero, there's plenty*
> > *to lose.*
> *You hope to recover a treasure once lost,*
> *But to gain such a treasure comes at what*
> > *cost?"*

Poppy sighs heavily. "Seriously, this Hermes dude needs a little positivity in his life! Talk about spinning something good into something so negative. That's him saying you passed the first test, right? You had the chance to get on that other train home, but you didn't."

"Yes, I think so. She remained in pursuit of the shield," Finn agrees. "The first challenge listed was Pursuit."

"Ella, you passed the first test!" Poppy exclaims. "Why is that poem so ... *sad*?"

"Because Hermes is making sure I know that was the easy part," I say, raking my fingers through my hair. "Finn, do you remember the order of the next challenges."

"Uh, yes," he confesses. "After Pursuit, it is Confusion, Panic, Fear and Fate."

"Huh," I say, nodding slowly. "Sounds fun."

"Confusion, Panic, Fear and Fate," Poppy reels off.

"Sounds like the emotions I go through when Dad announces he's had a go at baking."

I can't help but laugh, and Finn joins in, too, his infectious cackle filling the carriage. I feel some of the weight lift and a spark of hope returns.

River remains silent all the way to Glasgow.

It's not easy to fly to Barra last minute, especially when the world is shutting down in light of the bouts of unbearable battle noise. The way to get there is a small plane that lands on the beach, and those flights are dependent on weather conditions. Although it's a nice day, the pilots are refusing to take a small plane out, just in case the noise happens again.

We've come so far, but without the plane, we can't get to the island – and it's such a specific plane that we need, one that can land on the beach. It seems like a slim chance that we're going to be able to speak to the pilots themselves, let alone persuade them to take us to Barra. I can understand why they've cancelled flights.

We're standing in Glasgow airport, wondering what on earth we're going to do, when River makes a suggestion: "I could charter a plane."

My jaw drops to the floor.

"You … *what*?" Poppy says in disbelief.

"I could charter the plane," he repeats quietly, and he's using the same bashful tone that he spoke in when we arrived at his house. "I have some … connections and we can try to persuade a pilot to take us over. If you want, we can make the call. We can do that, right, Irving?"

"Yes, of course, we can try," Irving says, as though River has just asked if we can buy a bag of crisps.

"You can just … make a call and get a plane?" Finn asks, sounding bewildered.

"Possibly. No promises, but there might be someone my parents know who can help us. I don't think there's another way we can get to Barra, and I want to help. So, I can see if there's a pilot willing to take us."

"It can't be any plane. It's a specific one that lands on the beach," Poppy remarks in a tone that sounds a little ungrateful to me.

"I know, but I'll do what I can." He pauses, before adding, "We have to try, right?"

"Yes! That would be *amazing*," I gush, beaming at him with a wide smile. "River, if you pull this off, I don't know how we'd ever be able to thank you!"

"You'd thank me by getting the shield and

stopping Homados," he says in a hushed voice. "What happened on the train, I ... I don't want to have to keep experiencing that."

"I know, but River, when it happens again, try everything you can to get hold of my hand," I remind him. "That way, the Eye of Horus could protect you, too."

River hesitates. "I'm not sure it would work for me."

"What? River, why would you say that?"

"Because we don't know each other that well. It's cool, Ella, don't worry about it," he says quietly. "Anyway, I should go make this call. I'll be back in a second."

I hear him walk away accompanied by Irving and Maisie lets out a whine.

"I know," I mutter to her, frowning.

"What was that about?" Poppy asks, sidling over to me.

"River doesn't think the Eye of Horus would protect him," I explain. "I don't understand why he thinks that. Do you think he doesn't believe in it?"

"Ella, he's come all this way after hearing a couple of mythological stories, and he's witnessed an ancient tactile map moving and changing for you. I think he believes that things like the Eye of Horus exist and work just fine," she points out drily. "But he knows *how* it works. That's the problem."

"I'm lost. What do you mean?"

"Lugh told you that the Eye of Horus protects you and the people you *love*. I'm your sister and Finn's been your best friend a long time. But you barely know River. Are you even proper friends yet?"

"Yes! I mean, *I* thought so."

"Maybe River doesn't want to put that to the test," she reasons. "It would be a little awkward if it works for everyone but him, but also understandable. We don't *know* him."

I frown at her. "Why did you say it like that? We *do* know him."

She hesitates. "Don't you think it's a bit strange that he's so happy to pay for this whole trip and do things like charter *planes* for us?"

I sigh in frustration. "Poppy, it's that kind of attitude that makes him embarrassed to help. Who cares if he's rich? All I care about is who he is as a person and so far, he's proven to me that he wants to help everyone in the same way we do. Why are you so cynical?"

"I am not cynical!" she replies defensively. "I'm trying to look out for you!"

172

I fold my arms crossly. "Are you jealous of our friendship?"

"*What?*"

"Because if you are, I think it's unfair, Poppy. You've been so busy with all your sports teams recently, you haven't had time for me, and it's not OK that you should be against me finding a new friend to hang out with."

She doesn't say anything for a moment, and then in a quiet voice, she says, "You think I haven't had *time* for you?"

I can tell that the comment has stung and I feel an instant pang of regret. I didn't mean it as sharply as it came out.

"Poppy, I—"

"Hey," River calls out, and I hear him rushing back over to us, "I found a plane! And a pilot who is happy to take us to Barra. He's ready to go when we are. What do you say? Are you happy to do this?"

"Very happy," Poppy answers coldly. "The sooner this is all over, the better."

As I hear her turn and march away from me as quickly as possible, Maisie whines and then snorts grumpily, her disappointment in the situation unmistakable.

CHAPTER FIFTEEN

Just a few hours later, as the small plane descends towards the beach of Barra, I grip the arm of my seat, my heart racing, my whole body tense. The others gasp in wonder as we prepare to land. I remember it, that feeling of sheer amazement as I peered out of the window to find the bottom of the plane almost skimming the water before the bumpy landing on the long stretch of sand.

"Welcome to Barra," the pilot announces, as he brings the plane to a stop, the whirring propellers winding down.

I hear a series of clangs as everyone unbuckles their seatbelt. Finn is rambling about how cool the plane landing was to Poppy who has to ask him to repeat everything he's said because she had her headphones on. They're both nervous. When Finn is scared, he talks a lot. When Poppy's anxious, she drowns out the rest of the world by listening to music through her headphones. River and Irving are up front with the pilot. I can't hear what they're saying, but I'm going to go ahead and guess that River's nervous, too.

We're finally here in Barra. This is where the challenges really begin.

Finn exits the plane first, leading the way for Maisie and me, making sure we get down the narrow steps on to the beach safely. I politely thank the pilot as we go, despite our rocky start – when we first arrived at the plane on the Glasgow runway, he told River that no dogs were allowed on his plane. River had to explain that Maisie was a guide dog while I stood awkwardly, and the pilot said, "Oh. I *suppose* that's OK. We'll make sure we do a good hoover of the plane afterwards."

As Maisie carefully led me up the steps of the plane, I wondered whether that pilot was made to feel like an inconvenience when he tried to make his way around, feeling frightened and worried, during the Day of Darkness.

"River, I think I need to give you a warning,"

the pilot says once we're all off the plane and on the beach. "This fog is getting heavier. You were lucky we could land OK, and I need to take off quickly before it affects visibility. I know you were desperate to come here, and I'm happy to have been of service – but unless you come back now, I have to warn you that it won't be easy to get off this island."

"We can't go back now," River tells him.

"Then I hope you and your friends are prepared to be stuck here a while," the pilot says. "Are you sure about this?"

"We're sure," River answers.

"All right, it's your decision," the pilot says, unconvinced. "Good luck to you."

"Thanks, I think we'll need it," Finn mutters quietly.

Maisie guides me across the uneven sandy beach to the airport – a very small building from what I can remember – which is currently closed.

"Argh, I was hoping to get some snacks," Poppy grumbles, knocking and shaking the door handle. "You think we could use your lockpicker pen-thing, River?"

"We're not breaking into Barra airport to get snacks," I say, getting the map out of my pocket. "We

have to get going and you had some food at Glasgow Airport."

"Yeah, but quests make me hungry," she sighs. "I spent most of the Day of Darkness daydreaming about pastries. Do you know how hard it is to take down stone gargoyles when all you can think about is a doughnut?"

"Let's hope we don't meet any gargoyles this time round, then," I say, unfolding the map as my pendant grows warm.

"There's a symbol appearing on it," Finn points out. "What is that?"

"It's ... a castle," I say, running my fingers over the raised lines of the illustration.

Of course.

"Hey, there's a medieval castle here!" Poppy exclaims. "We visited it last time. Do you remember, Ella?"

"I remember," I mutter quietly, frowning.

Poppy waits a moment, probably studying my expression, before she asks, "Ella, why are we here? Why Barra? I don't remember anything frightening happening. I know it was a difficult time and that's why Mum and Dad wanted to bring us here to have a weekend away – obviously there were some bad moments, but nothing *frightening* happened to us there did it? We had a good time. That's how I remember it."

"Well, you would," I snap much harsher than I meant to. I sigh, adding, "Sorry, I didn't mean... Let's focus on getting to the castle."

"Do you remember where it was?" River asks.

"It was on another island of its own," Poppy mutters, still smarting from my tone.

"An island off an island?" River checks, amused. "Really?"

"Yeah," I say, sliding the map back into the pocket. "Kisimul Castle, the castle in the sea. It's off the south of the island."

"Great. What side of the island are we on now?" River asks.

"The north."

Finn sighs. "That's not a great start."

"We'll get a taxi," Poppy says. "There's one over there. Come on."

As I instruct Maisie to go forward, I already feel apprehensive about what the taxi driver will say about dogs and the fight that might be on our hands, but thankfully she doesn't hesitate to let us in, even going so far as to check where Maisie and I would be most comfortable. She introduces herself as Elsie and her cheerful welcome to Barra fills my stomach with a warmth that I was in need of. After mine and Poppy's argument at Glasgow airport and then the pilot's wary greeting, I've felt uneasy. The kindness of a stranger has helped me relax a little.

"I'll try to get you to Castlebay as quickly as I can," Elsie declares, as we pull away from the airport. "This fog is descending fast, I've never seen anything like it! Soon the roads won't be safe, and I have to tell you, I'm not sure the boat will be going across to the island."

"We'll find a way," I tell her stubbornly.

She wasn't kidding when she said she'd go as fast as she can. I have to feel for the grab handle and hold on to it for dear life as we're swung from side to side, hurling round the corners of the endless winding road. I even hear Irving gasp in fright at one point, which says a lot considering his usually stoic nature.

"B-Barra is so b-beautiful," River says, his voice wobbling from the potholes we're barrelling through at full speed. "So v-vast and qu-quiet."

"Yes, very peaceful," Elsie responds, before beeping the horn and yelling at the top of her lungs, "OUT OF THE ROAD, SEAGULL!"

At least we'll be at Castlebay quickly, but after a while the car begins to slow until it stops altogether and I know that, even at the speed Elsie was going, we can't be there yet.

"What is it?" I ask, sitting up straight. "What's wrong?"

"The fog is *so bad*," Finn tells me. "We can barely see anything."

"I can't drive any more in this," Elsie says apologetically.

"Oh dear," Irving says, sounding relieved.

"We have to turn back," Elsie continues, oblivious to Irving's tone. "I know the roads back much better. We can go very slowly. There's a hotel right by my house you can stay until it lifts. They serve good fish there!"

"No, we have to get to Castlebay," I say.

"Ella, no one will drive in this fog," Poppy informs me. "I can't even see the road any more. It's so thick, I don't think I've ever seen fog like this!"

"It wasn't forecast. I suppose you can never quite tell what you're going to get in Barra," Elsie chuckles.

"We can walk," Irving declares, and I hear him open the door.

"Thanks, Elsie, you turn back and get home safe. We'll get out here," I decide.

"Are … are you sure?" she says in surprise. "You're in the middle of the countryside here, it's a hilly walk to Castlebay."

"We'll be fine, thank you," I assure her.

She seems reluctant to drop us where we are, but we're already climbing out of the car and eventually she has to accept our decision, wishing us the best and turning her car round slowly to crawl back the way she came.

"Are you all right, Irving?" River asks. "You look a bit green in the face."

"A little carsick, sir, that's all," Irving says breathlessly, and I hear him stumble, clearly wobbly on his feet after the experience of Elsie's reckless driving.

"This is not a good idea," Poppy states, as we make our way further into the field, out of the way of the road. "Ella, I don't think you understand how bad this fog is."

"*Argh!*"

I stop at Irving's cry that's followed by a soft thud as something hits the grass, spinning round to face him. "What's happened?"

"Irving fell over!" River says. "Are you OK, Irving?"

"That looked bad," Finn comments grimly.

"I think … I think I've sprained my ankle, sir," Irving replies, sounding pained.

"Can you walk on it?" Poppy asks anxiously.

"Here, lean on me," River offers.

I hear Irving yelp in pain as he attempts to stand.

"No, no, it's no good," he says through wheezes. "It's too painful!"

"Oh Irving, I'm so sorry," I say, biting my lip.

"What are we going to do?" Finn asks. "You can't walk in this fog, Irving, you might make the injury even worse. We'll go get help."

"No, you have to go on," Irving insists in a strained voice. "The noise … you must stop it. You've come this far; you can't delay now."

"But we can't leave you here," River says.

"I'll be fine," he insists. "I'll sit for a moment and wait for the fog to lift. When it does, I'll be able to call for help. I have Elsie's card. I'll phone her when it's safe to drive again and she can pick me up." I hear him gulp loudly. "Or perhaps she can recommend a colleague."

"Irving—"

"River, this is important," Irving cuts in, his voice more serious than I've heard him use before. "You have to keep going. I'll be *fine*."

After taking a moment to weigh up the options, River relents. "All right, if you're sure. You promise you'll be OK?"

"If you promise the same," Irving replies.

"We'll look after him," I assure Irving. "That, *I* can promise."

River doesn't say anything, but Irving thanks me.

"OK, so we're carrying on," Poppy confirms. "How do we work out which way to go from here?"

"By using the tools that Hermes has provided." I crouch down to lay the map out on the grass and fish the compass out of my bag.

"I can understand why Lord Almond thought that was something astrological with its weird markings. That compass doesn't *look* like a compass," Finn observes.

I feel across the surface of it and break into a smile. "It's like a Bradley watch."

"A what?" River says, puzzled.

"A Bradley watch," I repeat. "It uses magnetized ball bearings that move around it to indicate to the raised markers lining the edge. I can feel which direction we're meant to go by how the ball bearings are positioned."

"That's *awesome*," River says enthusiastically.

"The compass is personalized for you, just like the map," Finn concludes, sounding impressed. "You really are the one who's meant to do this, Ella."

I press my lips together, not sure how to respond. I don't exactly feel good enough to be the one that the world is relying on, but I don't have a choice. Maisie, who is sitting next to me, rests her head in my lap and I smile, stroking her head.

You're always enough in my eyes, she's saying.

"The map is moving," Poppy observes, and I run my fingers across it to read what it's telling me.

"It's showing us the way to go," I announce, breaking into a smile as I feel the outline of four people and a dog right in the centre of the map. "OK, so this is where we are." I pause to touch the outlines of the landmarks and pathways that are appearing beneath my fingertips, marvelling at the way it feels, as though someone is illustrating them for me at this very moment as I feel my way across the map. "There's a church here, and that must be a campsite there. And over here we have some kind of … lake, I think. OK, so from here we want to go in a south-east direction."

I stand up, holding the compass out in the palm of my hand. I feel the ball bearings spin round as I move to point it south.

"Got it! We need to go this way," I declare, pointing ahead of me.

"Right, let's go," River says eagerly.

"Hang on," Poppy says, and I hear the crinkle of the parchment as she picks the map up from the ground. "That can't be right."

I drop my hand. "What do you mean?"

"Before the fog got so bad, I could see the spire of the church that's marked here," she claims. "And the way you've pointed to doesn't match to where I saw it in relation to this." She taps at the map. "Either the compass isn't working or you're reading it wrong."

I frown and then feel for the raised markers next to the ball bearings.

"I'm not reading it wrong," I state. "And I doubt that the compass is broken."

"It must be," Poppy says loftily.

"Poppy, this is a compass created by a god," I remind her.

"A god that likes to play tricks," she counters. "Maybe he's doing that to you now."

"He wants us to get to the castle so we can meet our next challenge," I say, growing frustrated. "So, he's not going to send us the wrong way. The

186

compass is right, and so is the map." I gesture in the direction I pointed to before. "We need to go this way."

"I'm telling you, I saw where the church was before the fog got bad, and the direction you want to go in does not make sense if you want to get to Castlebay."

"Poppy, I think we should follow the map and the compass rather than what you thought you saw, OK? Let's go."

"What I *thought* I saw?" she repeats, her temper flaring. "You think I'm making this up!"

"No," I say earnestly. "But if the map and compass are telling us to go *this* way, don't you think we should probably go with that direction? It would be easy for you to have got a bit confused with the fog coming down so quickly and we have walked off from the road. Maybe you're getting mixed up."

"I am not getting mixed up!" she protests. "Why won't you listen to me?"

"I *am* listening to you! I get what you're saying, but I've read the compass and map correctly, and they match up to go this way."

"And I'm telling you that something is wrong. I

am not going in that direction, because that will not take us to Castlebay."

I clench my jaw at her stubbornness. *Why is she so annoying?*

"You're saying you are *refusing* to come this way, then, even though that's where the map and compass are telling us to go," I clarify.

"That's right. I'm going the opposite direction. The *right* direction."

"It's the wrong way, Poppy!"

"No, it's not, Ella!"

"You know what? We don't have time for this. You go whichever way you want."

"Yes, I will," she huffs.

"Fine. You go that way and we'll go this way."

"Fine!"

"*Fine!*"

"Hang on," Finn says, as I check the compass again and prepare myself to follow it, listening to Poppy crinkling the map as she checks her position. "You're splitting up?"

"Apparently," I say, lifting my chin.

"But the fog is so bad now, I can barely see you in front of me," he says.

"We'll see who's right," Poppy mutters, ignoring

him. "I look forward to your apology, Ella, when I'm at the top of the castle and you're in the middle of some farmyard with a bunch of cows."

"It's called a *herd*, Poppy."

"That's not my point, Ella!"

"OK, let's calm down," Finn cuts in nervously. "With the fog being this thick, we should stick together, don't you think?"

"Yeah, I don't think we should split up," River agrees. "The map and compass only work if they're together anyway, remember? Ailynn told us that."

"Ailynn was wrong. The map is working fine," Poppy says and I hear her marching away before she calls back, "Yep! Still working fine all the way from over here. Guess it works for people who know how to read it correctly."

"Argh!" I huff. "If you're going to be like this, Poppy, that's your choice. Maisie and I are going this way. River, are you coming?"

"I ... uh ... yeah, OK," he says, baffled.

"Fine, in that case, Finn, you're coming with me," Poppy yells without giving him the option. "That's fair. We'll see who gets to Castlebay first. Finn, follow the sound of my voice! I'm over here! Come on, we don't have time to lose."

"Good luck following her through the fog, Finn," I mutter bitterly.

"I heard that and I'm good at walking in the dark, actually, Ella," she calls out. "It was you who taught me how, remember?"

I purse my lips as I hear her instruct Finn to hold on to her shoulder, before she storms away in the other direction. Maisie emits a sad whine that carries across the field. Poppy must be able to hear it. But she doesn't come back.

CHAPTER SIXTEEN

I march on determinedly through the grass with River's hand resting on my shoulder. Maisie guides me carefully over the unsteady field until we reach a pathway heading in the right direction.

"She is so unbelievably stubborn," I remark, having complained solidly about Poppy for the last few minutes since we parted ways. "How can she believe that she's right but a compass and map are wrong?"

"I think that—" River begins timidly, but I cut across him.

"And not just any compass and map! The compass and map of *Hermes*. A god! Poppy thinks she has a better sense of direction than a *god*. This is the girl who once got lost walking across Tower Bridge. Have you been to Tower Bridge, River?"

"Uh … yeah."

"And you know how bridges work?"

"Yes."

"They literally go from one side of the river to the other. In one straight line. So, *how* does someone get lost walking from one side of Tower Bridge to the other?"

"I have no idea," he sighs.

"No, neither do I. But somehow Poppy did."

"Ella, maybe we should—"

"I bet she knew I was making a good point about the compass and the map, but she didn't want to admit that," I mutter crossly. "She is so stubborn and it's …"

I trail off as I hear a familiar voice coming from up ahead and getting closer.

"… and to be honest, Finn, I think she might be the most stubborn person I ever met."

I bring Maisie to a stop, causing River to trip over his feet as he halts behind me.

"*Poppy?*" I call out, listening intently.

"Ella?" she replies, her voice right in front of me now. "How did you get here?"

"How did *you* get here?"

"How did you *all* get here?" Irving asks, sounding bewildered on the grass near us.

"Oh, I get it, Ella," Poppy says triumphantly. "You realized I was right and followed me!"

"I was about to accuse you of the same thing!" I exclaim, astounded at her refusal to admit she was in the wrong. "I can't believe you'd rather lie than admit I was right."

"I'm not lying about anything! You're the one who's followed me."

"Why would I follow you when you were going the wrong way?" I ask pointedly. "You have been following me and can't admit it."

"That is not true!"

"Since Irving hasn't moved, I think we must have gone in a circle," Finn says from behind Poppy.

"I think we might have done the same," River adds wearily at my shoulder.

"I agree," Irving says.

Maisie grunts.

I quickly feel for the bearings on the compass, realizing that I was so busy complaining about Poppy that I haven't been checking it as often as I should've done. Clearing my throat, I lift my chin defiantly.

"No, we're exactly where I thought we were," I insist. "Come on, River, we're going straight from here."

"And we're going straight from here," Poppy says, and I hear her sidestep me to move round us.

"You're still determined to go the wrong way then?" I check.

"Don't call me in a panic when you find yourselves back at the airport while we've been chilling at the castle for hours having a lovely time," she counters.

"I'm not sure a lovely time is waiting for anyone at the castle," Finn notes grimly.

Ignoring them, I give Maisie her instruction and we start walking, River sighing heavily behind me but loyally sticking on my team. I've decided to forgive Finn for going with Poppy, because he didn't have much of a choice and also he's going to have a miserable time wandering for hours in the wrong direction. That's punishment enough.

"She is unbelievable," I mutter under my breath. "All she has to do is put her hands up and admit that she got it wrong, then poor Finn wouldn't be walking in circles."

"We also walked in a circle," River comments.

"That's not important," I say, bristling. "We may have gone a bit off course, but we're on the right path now – I've double checked the compass."

"We could wait for the fog to lift."

"No way, River, we don't have time."

"I think it's better than splitting up. I thought you were meant to be a team."

I frown but don't say anything. Instead, I focus on checking the compass to make sure that we're on the right course, something I'm absolutely sure of until…

"… and you know what else, Finn? She can't even admit she's wrong."

"You said that already," Finn sighs. "Three times."

We come to a stop again as their voices approach from the path directly ahead of us.

"Hello again," Irving says wearily from just metres away. "I see you haven't got far."

"Poppy, you are *kidding*," I accuse loudly. "You don't have to keep following us secretly. You can admit that you've changed your mind."

"How did you get there?" Poppy demands to know, standing right in front of me.

"You know how! You've obviously realized that I'm right and you're wrong."

"*You've* obviously realized that *I'm* right and *you're* wrong," she retorts, flustered.

"I think we're back to where we started," River comments.

"You're right!" Finn says. "How did that happen?"

"You mean we've been going round in circles again?" I check, putting my hand on my hip. "That can't be right, River, I've been checking the compass."

"And I've been checking the map," Poppy claims. "We've been walking the exact way I planned to."

"So have we, and—" I stop as I feel the ball bearings move round the compass. "Oh. Uh … hang on. We're meant to be going the opposite way."

"Aha!" Poppy cries in victory. "That's exactly what I— Oh. Hang on. I'm looking at the map and I think … I think we're meant to be going the opposite way. Yep, we need to turn round, Finn. Back the way we came!"

"Us too," I tell River.

"Hang on, so even though you were both wrong that time, we're still not walking the same way?" Finn groans. "This doesn't make sense!"

"It makes *perfect* sense, Finn," Poppy insists. "Come on, let's go."

With Finn muttering something inaudible under his breath, the two of them set off the wrong way while Maisie and I turn to head back along the path we've just come down. River stays with us, but I can tell that he's getting impatient, and my confidence in my compass-reading abilities is starting to sway.

"We're going the right way this time," I declare, trying to convince myself as much as him. "I think the compass needed a little time to warm up."

"I don't think that's how compasses work," he says.

"Positive thinking, River," I say boldly, nodding as we march onwards. "Soon we'll hear the sound of the waves as we get closer to the coast and then all we'll need to do is persuade someone to take us on a boat out to the castle."

"I definitely can't hear waves."

"Not yet, but soon."

"The fog isn't lifting and all I see beneath my feet is this dusty path we've been on the entire time. I don't think we've even made it out of the first field yet."

"Which makes perfect sense according to my plans," I say, but not even *I* think I sound believable. "Any minute now we'll be at the harbour."

My pace slows as I hear a sound that makes me deflate: "Trust me, Finn, any minute now we'll be right by the boats."

"Reunited again!" Irving says from somewhere nearby, sounding amused.

"No!" I cry out, as I hear Poppy and Finn approach us. "This isn't possible! Are you doing this on purpose, Poppy?"

"No! You're the one doing this! I'm walking where I'm meant to according to the map!" I hear her shake the parchment in the air.

"If this is some kind of joke, then it isn't funny," I say, scowling. "You're wasting precious time!"

"I'm not doing anything, Ella! You're the one who keeps getting in my way."

"No, *you're* the one who—"

"That's enough!" cries Finn, stunning us both into silence.

It's rare that Finn ever raises his voice. Maisie seems to be in agreement with him as she plonks her bottom down to sit stubbornly at my feet and snorts in protest, refusing to move until we've sorted this mess out.

"I'm tired of you both bickering and leading us in circles," Finn says.

"Me too," River adds.

"I didn't mean to lead you in circles, River," I point out. "I was using the compass."

"Same, I was following the map," Poppy says, her voice softening.

"And I believe both of you, but something is going wrong," Finn says, tiredly.

"Isn't Hermes a trickster god?" River notes. "Could

this be his plan? What if it seems like the map and the compass are working when separated, when they're not?"

Finn gasps. "Of course. That's it!"

"What?" I ask urgently. "What have you realized?"

"Confusion," he says simply, as though that should answer it for us. When no one reacts, he realizes he needs to embellish: "The next challenge after Pursuit is *Confusion*. I don't know about you but I'm confused right now."

I grip the compass tighter, feeling betrayed by it. "You mean we're facing the next challenge already? Without even knowing it?"

"The unusual, peculiar fog. The map not matching Poppy's sight of landmarks. Walking in circles and always ending up at the start no matter which way we turn." Finn starts chuckling as though it's funny. "It all makes sense!"

"So how are we going to get out of this?" Poppy asks. "If we keep coming back to the start, how are we going to find where we need to be?"

"I don't know, but I think we have a better chance of finding the correct path out of here if we work as a team," River suggests. "We've got this far by doing that, haven't we?"

"You're right, River. I'm in. What do you two think?" Finn prompts.

Poppy doesn't say anything. Neither do I for a moment. Then I realize that it wasn't Poppy's fault after all. She may have been right about the landmarks not matching the map. Hermes set it up that way. I probably shouldn't have dismissed her so quickly.

"Fine. Yes, I think we should work as a team."

"Me too," Poppy says.

"Good. OK, so –" Finn exhales – "anyone have any thoughts on how to overcome confusion?"

"Well, I think I might," I offer. "When I first lost my sight, I'd often feel confused. It could be really overwhelming. It was stressful and I felt disorientated. It was confusing to have to re-learn how to do things that I used to be able to do without thinking about it. Some of the hardest challenges were completing what should be easy tasks. I remember talking to Gavin about it a lot."

"Who's Gavin?" River asks.

"He was my mobility instructor. He helped me to navigate my environment safely, so I could do things independently. Things like making a cup of tea or crossing the street or even getting out of bed and finding my way across my room." I allow a weak smile. "You don't realize how much you do without thinking. I had to learn all of that again."

"That does sound confusing," River admits.

I nod slowly. "It was. Gavin would tell me that it's OK to feel confused, though. It was OK to feel frustrated, but that didn't mean I was failing. I had to take a deep breath, allow myself a pause and take the time to accept the situation and how I feel about it. Then, I could work out what I can control and go from there."

I hear Finn take a confident step forward. "I think that's good advice. Let's all hold hands and take a deep breath together. Maisie, you're involved in this, too – I'll put my foot up against your paw so you know you're in the circle."

River takes my free hand in his, while Finn places his hand over my other hand holding Maisie's harness.

"Deep breath in," Finn instructs, leading the charge. "And deep breath out. Very good. Let's do that again all together."

We keep to his calm rhythm of breaths. Already I feel a weight lift, as though my heart was being weighed down by an anger that's starting to evaporate, expelled from my body with each long exhale.

"Great," Finn says, satisfied after a few more group breathing exercises. "I think we've all accepted that we're very confused right now, but that's OK, right?"

"Yeah, it won't last forever," River notes, his voice light and amused.

"We *will* find our way out of this," Poppy states, and I believe her.

"We will," I echo. "Poppy, I think you should lead the way. If that doesn't work, then I can read the compass again and we can try another way. Whatever we do, let's stick together. Like River has reminded us, we're a team. That's the most important thing."

"Thanks, Ella," she says softly, and I can hear that she's smiling. "But if I'm honest, I've lost my bearings a bit. I might lead us the wrong way."

"I think you should have more faith in your abilities," I say, holding out the compass for her to take.

But my hand knocks against hers and I realize that she's held out the map to give it over to me at the exact same time.

Finn suddenly gasps. "Wait! There's a light! It's a lamp post!"

"That wasn't there before," Poppy says, shocked.

"It's lighting the path," River tells me. "There's another lamp further down that's lit up, too. And more beyond it!"

"The compass is moving," I say, feeling it whir in my hands, the ball bearings spinning round and round before they come to a stop.

"And the map is changing," Poppy says excitedly. "Ella, here, take the map and check with the compass which way we're supposed to go."

"It's as though the light from the lamps is lifting the fog," River says with wonder.

"I think you might be right," Finn laughs, as I check the compass against the map. "We can see the whole field now. And the road over there!"

"According to the map and compass, I think we need to go this way," I say, pointing in a direction as I double check where the ball bearings have landed.

"Yes! There's the church in the distance, exactly where it should be according to the map!" Poppy squeals, clapping her hands. "Finally, it makes sense! You're right, Ella. Let's go before it all changes again."

"Hey, Irving," River says, and it sounds like he's smiling.

"I see you got far without me, sir."

"Now we can see where we're going, let's help you to Castlebay. There should be a doctor there who can help," River suggests, crouching down to help Irving up.

"Hang on, the landmarks on the map are fading and there's more Braille," I announce, my fingertips at the ready to read it. "It's another poem."

"What does it say?" Finn asks, and I read it out:

"Confusion is not a war or a race,
But a strand in our stories that we all
> *must face.*
Acceptance, humility, I find help it to dim,
Your choices are clearer when you're
> *brighter within.*

Two tests are behind you, more ahead
> *should you choose,*
Your pathway is clear now, not a moment
> *to lose.*
With your friends at your side, you stand
> *in good stead,*
But patience, shield-seeker, rough seas lie
> *ahead."*

CHAPTER SEVENTEEN

The crossing to Kisimul Castle from Barra is just five minutes. There's a small boat that usually leaves from Castle Slip Landing, round the corner from the marina, but when we get there, tired from a lot of hillside walking, the ramp to the boat is closed.

"The sign says there are no more crossings until further notice," Finn says, defeated.

"Elsie warned us this might happen," Poppy recalls. "It's the fog."

"Can you see the castle? From what I remember, it's not far from here, sitting on its own little island in the sea," I say.

"The fog is too heavy to see anything past the railings," River tells me. "The lamps may have helped to light our way here, but they've disappeared now."

"There's no one to ask about the crossing," Finn adds. "It's so quiet."

"Is there a café or pub around here?"

"I think we may have passed a hotel on our way down," River tells me. "I could make out the sign from the road."

"Let's start there," I suggest. "Someone might be able to help us and we can try to get help for Irving. We only need one person with a boat willing to do the short crossing. Surely there's going to be someone in this town who wants to help."

With a fresh wave of determination, we make our way back up the road to the hotel overlooking the bay. I hear poor Irving grunt with pain as we set out again, River and Finn helping him along. He hasn't complained at all, only admitting to "some minor discomfort" when pressed, but it's been a lot of walking since his injury.

As soon as we step through the door of the hotel, I can sense a gloomy atmosphere in this building. Maisie gives a small whine as she stops in reception. I can hear the sound of people in here – fingers tapping on phones, newspapers crinkling as the pages are turned, the local news playing on a TV in the top back corner, glasses being placed down on coasters – but no one is talking to each other. There's no laughter or music or joy here.

While River goes to help Irving sit down at one of the tables, I take off Maisie's harness for a bit, since she's had to work hard with all the travelling today and the long walk to Castlebay. I also get the feeling that I might not be the only one she'll be able to bring some comfort to in here. I want to give people the chance to stroke and fuss her if they need. As I take off her harness, she shakes and then immediately sniffs at my hand and licks it, as though thanking me for a little break.

Already she's made me smile.

"Hello," someone greets us from behind the reception desk, sounding confused at our arrival. "Can I help you?"

"Hi, I hope so," I say brightly, hoping that a warm, positive attitude will help our cause. "We'd like to visit Kisimul Castle. Can you point us in the right direction of finding someone to take us on a boat across to the island?"

"Sorry, the castle's closed. All crossings cancelled until further notice."

"Can I ask why?" I say politely.

"The fog. No one will take a boat out in this weather."

"Do you think someone might make an exception?" I check. "It doesn't have to be the official boat that goes to the castle, we'd be happy to hitch a lift with a fishing boat or anyone who'd be willing to let us tag along."

"But *none* of the boats are going out," he emphasizes. "It's too dangerous."

I lower my voice, leaning across the counter conspiratorially. "Is there anyone you can think of who we might be able to persuade? I wouldn't ask if it wasn't important."

"You want to visit the castle that badly?"

"There's something there that we need. It can't wait."

"I'm afraid it will have to," he says, sucking air in through his teeth. "The thing is, normally I would have suggested a couple of names to you, but with the way things are here at the moment, I don't think anyone is going to help you. There's a lot of … anger."

"What do you mean?" Poppy asks, intrigued. "Is this something to do with the noise?"

"Aye," he says in a low voice. "Usually this place is buzzing, we have a band that plays live music – but they've all fallen out. That's one of them over there in the corner with the broken violin. He did that when he threw it at the fella on the drums." He sighs, tutting. "A few of our locals have been friends for years, but now they're sworn enemies. It was a small but lively community here up until a few days ago. Not any more."

"That's so sad," I comment, my heart sinking.

"What's sad is that people don't listen when I tell them what's going on here," someone with a gruff voice interjects, sitting on a table to my right. "No one will listen. You know what I believe? This isn't the work of the government or a corporation, this is the work of the gods!"

"Don't mind him," the receptionist mutters. "He's always like this, rambling on about old folktales and stories, full of nonsense. No one believes any of it."

"Wait, what did you say?" I ask, turning towards the gruff voice. "What do you mean this is the work of the gods?"

"He's trying to upset you," remarks the receptionist irritably. "He likes the attention. Don't listen to him."

"The loud unbearable noise that makes us full of rage," the man says in answer to my question. "You ask me, a god is playing games with our world. That noise is indoors, outdoors, wherever you go – it's in *our heads.* I was out on the boat when I heard it first, right in the middle of the sea."

"We've told you, Andrew, the technology these companies have would blow your mind," the receptionist snaps back. "They'd be able to reach you out there."

Andrew snorts indignantly. "On an old fishing boat?"

"It has radio, doesn't it? You're not going to scare us with your old folktales and fairytales," the receptionist says sternly. "You've already annoyed your friends with this talk." He sighs, before addressing us to say, "Andrew here likes to regale tourists with mythological stories in the hope of adding a touch of magic to the place. But now he talks as though he thinks what he's saying is fact. For him, the line between fairytale and reality has become blurred. It's *embarrassing.*"

"I believe that what's embarrassing is us humans acting as though we know everything there is to know about everything," Andrew seethes. "Some things can't be explained and, if you ask me, there's just as much evidence that some mythical being or god could be behind something as powerful as this."

"Well, we didn't ask you, did we?" the receptionist

snaps. "You're always trying to butt in where you're not wanted. Your head is filled with pointless stories and you're—"

"This isn't you, Jack," Andrew says sharply. "Whatever is going on has been making you rude and irritable. You never used to talk to me like this."

My pendant begins to grow warm against my neck.

"You don't know me!" Jack counters haughtily. "You don't know anything about—"

He stops talking, before emitting a high-pitched "*No!*"

I hear a clatter from behind the counter as though he's thrown himself down behind it as he starts whimpering.

The familiar clashing of metal and the faint cries and shouts of men grow louder.

"The noise, it's happening again," Andrew declares in a terrified whisper. "Try not to lose yourselves! Fight against the urge to hate on your fellow men!"

"River, *no!*" Finn cries to my other side.

"What is it?" I ask him frantically.

"He's gone to shut himself away in the toilet," Finn says, as he takes my hand and Poppy reaches for the other. "I couldn't stop him!"

"We need to reach him."

"It's too late," Poppy says, her voice shaking as the noise escalates.

It's getting worse. Even the Eye of Horus can't protect us fully from its power. My head is filled with the din of battle: scraping metal that covers my skin in goosebumps and sends a shiver down my spine, the sharp whistle of soaring weapons that makes my eyes water. But above all else the cries and shouts of people fighting for their lives.

"Make it *stop*," Poppy says through sniffles, her fingernails digging into the skin of my arm. "It's hurting everyone."

Her observation is supported by the shrieks of everyone surrounding us as they grapple with the horror filling their ears, before random arguments begin popping up across the room. The receptionist starts yelling at the violinist he mentioned to us just moments ago; a woman somewhere is shouting at her partner for stealing her chips all the time; and most terrifyingly, someone is bellowing across the room at us, blaming the painful noise on "young kids and teenagers trying to brainwash the rest of us".

Maisie whines, leaning against me.

Lurking beneath the din of armour smashing and

roars of fury and fearful cries is that spine-chilling, eerie cackle that grows louder and louder, causing my heart to race.

"Can … can anyone else hear that?" I ask breathlessly.

"Yes! Everyone can hear the noise, Ella!" Poppy says, bewildered.

"No, the laugh."

"What laugh?"

"*That* laugh!" I grimace as it roars in my ears. "He's laughing at us!"

"There's no laugh, Ella," Finn says, sounding worried. "We can't hear anyone laughing."

"Why would someone laugh at this?" Poppy croaks, sounding close to tears.

I shake my head, trying to shake his laugh right out of my ears.

"It's OK," I say determinedly. "It's going to be OK."

"It *will* be OK," I hear Andrew reply through gritted teeth, before he grunts with pain. "We … must … fight … this!"

"Andrew, can you hear me?" I cry in amazement, turning towards his voice.

He cries out in pain and I jump at the thud of a fist pounding on the table coming from his direction.

He's unable to respond to my question, but as the noise fades away, I am filled with hope. This man was fighting it without the help of the Eye of Horus. He may not have made it completely disappear, but he didn't lose himself completely.

And he did that by believing.

"I'm going to check on River," Finn says when the noise has gone completely.

"I think that's a good idea," Poppy tells him, sounding anxious as the room descends into furious rows. "We need to get out of here, Ella."

"Where's that guy – Andrew? The one who spoke to us about the gods?" I ask.

"He's on a table by himself. He almost smashed it in two, but he's not yelling at anyone. He's got his head in his hands," she says quietly.

"I need to speak to him," I say, and she doesn't question it, taking my arm and leading me over to his table.

"Hi, Andrew," Poppy begins, clearing her throat to grab his attention. "Are you OK?"

"I will be," he says grimly. "What do you want?"

"We happen to *know* that this is the work of the gods," I say bluntly. "It's the work of one god in particular. Have you ever heard of Homados?"

"The god of battle noise," he says, his tone laced with curiosity. "This is him, eh?"

"Yes, and we have a way to stop him. But we need to get to Kisimul Castle. You mentioned that you have a boat? I need you to take us there. Now."

"Kisimul Castle," he repeats. "Why there?"

"I … I can't tell you." I swallow the lump in my throat. "I need you to trust us."

"Even if I did, I couldn't help you get to the castle," he says, sounding regretful. "The fog is too thick and heavy. It's too dangerous to take anyone out there."

"Andrew, I think we were destined to meet you," Poppy jumps in confidently. "We've travelled all the way here from London, and it seems almost impossible that we have made it this far. But we're here and a few minutes ago, I thought we were all doomed. There didn't seem to be any hope we'd be able to complete this quest to Kissymore Castle—"

"*Kisimul* Castle," I correct.

"Whatever. The point is, Andrew, we walk in here, a bunch of kids looking for a boat, on a mission to stop a god and who do we meet? A local who has a boat and knows that this is the work of gods even though *no one else believes him*." She pauses

215

dramatically. "What do you call that, Andrew? Because I call that … *destiny*."

"I suppose it is all a bit odd," he notes.

I wince as someone roars at their companion behind me.

"Do you hear that? Your town is being ripped apart by this, and so is everywhere else," I point out. "Soon, Homados will have his way and everyone will be at war. It will be a world of chaos that he can easily rule without anyone able to oppose him. Will you help us stop him before it gets that far?"

"It's your destiny, Andrew," Poppy adds in a mystical voice.

I suppress a smile.

He exhales loudly. "If it's my destiny, I cannae ignore it."

"So we have ourselves a boat?" I ask hopefully, holding out my hand.

"Aye," he says, taking my hand and shaking it, "you've got yourselves a boat."

CHAPTER EIGHTEEN

I've always loved being out on the water.

We went to Ireland on holiday a few years ago before I lost my sight, and we took the ferry across – I remember feeling calm and mesmerized as I stood with Poppy by the rail on the deck, looking out across the sea that stretched on forever. As I sit on Andrew's fishing boat now with Maisie lying safely under my legs without her harness on, swaying gently side to side as we cut through the water, I listen to the splash of the waves hitting the sides of the boat and inhale the cold salty air. I'm captivated by that peaceful feeling all over again, and, after a tumultuous few days, it's like I can finally *breathe* out here.

I think I may be the only one, though. Finn didn't feel confident getting on the boat, informing me in a low, nervous voice that it was "a faded blue, about thirty foot long and looked old and rickety".

"She's a beauty, eh?" Andrew bellowed over the wind proudly as we climbed aboard.

His comment was greeted by a chorus of unenthusiastic "*mmmms*".

Finn is sitting towards the back of the boat with River. Before we left the hotel, Irving, who is staying there to rest his ankle until we get back, told us that River gets seasick. Andrew tried to encourage River to come up to the helm with him as he thought it might be better for him to look straight ahead like he was driving, but River said he preferred to be away from us in case he had to lean over the side to vomit.

"I think that's a good idea," Poppy agreed, not bothering to hide her disgust in her tone. "You go right to the back, River, keep going. As far away from me as possible. I'll sit up here at the front."

I told her off for being so unsympathetic, but she ignored me and when Andrew started regaling folktales of the area, I soon heard the distinctive, muffled sound of music playing through her headphones. Luckily, he didn't seem to notice or mind.

"There are a great many tales about these parts,"

Andrew declares to me, his captive audience of one. "Have you heard of kelpies?"

"Isn't that an Australian dog breed?"

He chuckles. "I'm talking about water kelpies from Scottish folklore. Mythical shape-shifting spirits of the water. They live in the lochs and seas here, and can take the form of horses or humans. They lure humans into the water."

"They don't sound very friendly."

"There was one, the Water Horse of Barra, who, legend has it, was tricked by a clever young woman. He ended up falling in love with her and became good." Andrew hesitates. "Of course, that was just the *one* kelpie. Not sure there's any others with stories that end so happily."

"Let's hope it's just … folklore, then."

"Sounds to me like you have experience with that sort of thing," Andrew notes. "It's nice to meet someone who appreciates that these stories don't come from nothing. You say that the god of battle noise is behind all this?"

"Homados."

"He's dangerous, I imagine."

"Yes, but I don't think kelpies are his thing," I point out, forcing a smile. "You'll be safe here on the

219

boat and when we get to the castle, you shouldn't come with us."

"I don't know about that, Ella Jones," he says in a gruff voice. "I've always known the waters here are magical. They draw you in. They have their own stories to tell."

We fall silent. The rudder shakes and creaks as we shift direction.

I bend forward to place a hand on Maisie's belly, using the steady rhythm of her breathing to calm me. I'm glad that Andrew has come to the end of his conversation. At first I was glad to have the distraction before we got to the castle, but now I'm looking forward to being on dry land. I remind myself of how far we've come as my confidence wobbles.

When I hear a noise in the distance, I tense until I realize that it's not the battle noise of Homados. It's so faint at first that I wonder whether it's Poppy's music, but I can still hear hers coming from her headphones too, so it can't be.

"What is that?" I ask Andrew, but he must be focusing on listening, trying to work out what it is too, because he doesn't answer.

As we get closer to the noise, I realize that it's a choir. A well-rehearsed choir with the most beautiful voices I've ever heard. The singing is so soothing, it makes me smile. I wonder if it's coming from the castle, puzzled as to why Andrew wouldn't mention that there was a choir to greet tourists as they arrived. If I lived somewhere with a choir this good, I'm not sure I'd be able to stop talking about it. Their voices make me feel happy and warm. They're so alluring that for a moment, I forget where I am and what we're doing and I lose myself in the song, feeling tranquil and safe.

I'm distracted from the music by the Eye of Horus growing warm on my neck. I place my fingertips on top of the pendant, frowning as it gets hotter and hotter beneath my touch. It doesn't make any sense – I can't hear the unbearable noise at all. Why is the Eye of Horus working to protect me and what would it be protecting me from?

Maisie sits up and whines, nudging at my leg. That's when I know something is wrong. It hits me that we've been on the water for much longer than we should've been. It's meant to be barely a five-minute crossing. Andrew must have got confused in the fog.

"Andrew, are we lost?" I ask.

No one answers.

"Andrew?" I repeat.

The boat jolts suddenly and I hear the creak of footsteps, as though people are moving across the boat, making it lean to one side. Steadying myself on the rail, I place a hand on Maisie's head as she leans against me.

"It's OK, Maisie," I assure her, sounding more confident than I feel. "Poppy, what's going on? Finn? River? *Hello!* What's happening?"

I get no response and the panic unfurling in my stomach grows, engulfing me. The choir is louder now, as though the singers are surrounding the boat, but we're not on land or anywhere near it as far as I can tell. I can hear the water slapping against the boat on all sides as we rock unsteadily.

"Hello?" I cry desperately. "Someone say something! What's going on?"

But I still don't get a reply from any of my friends. My heart is thumping so hard against my chest, my ears are ringing, and I grip the rail behind me as I start to feel dizzy from panic. Why isn't anyone saying anything? Can't they hear me? Why are they moving around the boat? The choir is getting louder and louder but their song isn't calming any more, it's grating and unnerving. I don't understand who is singing and how they're so close to the boat when we're in the middle of the sea!

Something Andrew said flits across my mind: *I've always known the waters here are magical. They draw you in. They have their own stories to tell.*

I gasp, my blood running cold. Kelpies may not be a Greek god's first port of call, but other mythological sea creatures might. The Eye of Horus is burning now against my skin as the chorus of beautiful, enchanting voices fills the air.

Sirens.

CHAPTER NINETEEN

Telling Maisie to stay where she is as the boat is knocked back and forth by the waves, I carefully push myself off my seat and stumble forward in the direction of the helm.

"Andrew?" I call out, gripping the side of the steering station. "Andrew, where are you? Are you there?"

He doesn't reply and when I reach for the wheel, I find it spinning out of control with no one manning it. It must have been his footsteps I heard pass me by earlier, lured away from the helm to the back of the boat. Taking the wheel, I do my best to hold it steady with one hand, the other feeling across the station at all the controls.

"I … I don't know what I'm doing," I shout to no

one, gripping the helm with both hands now, hoping that if I keep it straight then at least we won't be rocking so much.

My mind is racing as I fall into full-fledged panic mode. No one is commanding the boat, and none of my companions can hear me because of the sirens, and I don't know how bad the fog is at this point, or whether we're on course to crash or be stranded out at sea.

I'm clinging to the hope that everyone is still on the boat at least – I haven't heard any splashes or cries for help. Yet.

"Andrew!" I croak, despite my hope fading that my voice will get through the bewitching song of the sirens. "Poppy! Finn? River? Anyone! Someone, *please!*"

No one answers and my voice is carried away on the wind.

I've never felt so alone.

Thrown uncontrollably from side to side, I let go of the wheel since steadying it doesn't seem to be making any difference. Frantically clinging on to the side, I slide to sit down and press my fingers into my ears, desperately trying to shut out the song of the sirens as their voices shatter any calm thoughts and send tears streaming down my cheeks. Bringing my knees up to my chest, I rest my forehead against them, sobbing as I spiral into panic. There is no hope for this situation. I can't steer the boat. I don't know where my friends are or what they might do when they're under the spell of sirens. I don't know how to save them. The song is getting louder and louder until I can barely hear anything else.

"I don't know what to do," I admit, feeling like my throat is closing up.

My hands are trembling against my face as I keep my fingers up to my ears, my chest is tightening with every shaky, short breath I take and my heart is racing.

Then I feel warm hands wrap round my wrists.

I jump, slamming my head as I jolt back from them.

"Ella! Ella, is that you?" Poppy shouts over the song, but I can hardly hear her.

Relief floods through me as I grip her hands and pull her into me, wrapping both arms round her and holding her tight. Maisie must be able to hear us, because she's made her way over to be at my side too, nudging my hand with her snout until I stroke her head, her insistence at getting a fuss right now making me laugh through my tears.

Poppy is saying something in my ear, but I can't hear her. The song of the sirens is so loud it drowns out all other noise. She's growing frustrated and so am I as we desperately try to communicate. Then Poppy moves my hands to place them over hers as she signs, "I found you. It's OK. I'm here."

We both learnt tactile sign language when we were little because of Aunty Hazel, our deaf–blind great aunt. It's been a while since either of us practised it, so I think we might be a bit rusty, but it's clever thinking of Poppy to use it now. It's a way of communicating when you have both hearing loss and sight impairment.

With a rush of hope, I let her put her hands over mine as I reply, "Is everyone OK?"

"I don't know," she signs back. "The fog is so bad, I can't see. I've got my headphones on still. The others were all acting strangely."

Poppy places her hands over mine, ready to feel the shape and movement of the signs that I make. "There are sirens. They are singing in the water. The song is too loud for me to hear you."

"When the fog came down, Finn and River stood up and turned to look at the water. They were in a daze and smiling dopily, their eyes were glazed over.

227

Then Andrew left the wheel and came to stand next to them. I thought I saw something move in the water. Then the fog got so bad, I couldn't see anything."

"How do we save them?" I sign.

"We'll think of a way. Together," she signs in reply.

"I'm so scared," I sign, tears overflowing again as I admit it. "What do we do? It's all gone wrong. It's my fault."

"I'm here now, Ella, I found you, it's OK. You need to take a deep breath."

One of her hands leaves mine to reach out and hold the side of my face, her thumb wiping the tears off that cheek. "Breathe in with me." She takes one of my hands and places it at the top of my chest, helping me to feel the slow, controlled rhythm of her breath. "And now out," she signs with the hand still under my other. "That's it, I've got you. Another one, let's do this."

She repeats her slow, calming breathing several times and I breathe along with her, the heavy haze that was clouding my brain starting to lift. I can feel my heart rate slow a little and my chest loosen as I focus purely on breathing in and out.

"Better?" she asks.

"Yes," I sign back. "Thank you."

"It's OK. I'm not surprised you were panicking."

Panicking. I've been *panicking*. I knew I was, but until she said the word out loud, I hadn't understood. But now I do. The poem from Hermes comes rushing back to me:

> *"First, a Pursuit with those you hold dear,*
> *Then comes Confusion, Panic and Fear.*
> *But more is due to lie in wait,*
> *for it is then that you shall meet your*
> *Fate."*

We accepted Pursuit, we made our way through Confusion, and now I'm in the midst of Panic. It's the next challenge on Hermes's list.

"Panic!" Poppy signs. "That was the next task from Hermes! Do you think this is it?"

"Yes! This is panic."

As soon as I sign it, the song of the sirens quietens a little, as though the power of my realization has caused someone to turn down their volume.

"The song is quieter now," I communicate to Poppy.

"Can you hear me?" she asks cautiously.

"Yes!" I sign.

"OK, that's something. I can't see you still, and I don't want to take my headphones off," she says wisely. "Tell me what you need me to do, Ella. We can complete this challenge together, I promise. We've done it before."

She didn't need to say that, though, because I already know. Ever since she found me crouched in this corner, alone and on the brink of giving up, I've known that it's going to be OK. The Eye of Horus may be able to protect me from the work of gods, but it can't protect me from myself, and for a moment, I lost who I was. I allowed Hermes to send me into a spiral of panic and forget that I have the strength to find my way out of it. I just needed reminding of that. I needed Poppy to remind me.

This is not the first time I've panicked. I'm usually quite a calm, confident person, but it's happened a *lot*. When I was last here in Barra, I was panicking about what was to come and what my world was going to turn into. Then when that time came and I lost my eyesight, I panicked about everything: my future, my lifestyle, what I had lost, who I was going to be. It was Gavin who helped me to cope with the onset of panic. He told me how important breathing was and how to use grounding techniques like focusing on my other senses: what I could hear, smell, taste at the time to help calm me. But whether she meant to or not, it's Poppy who has given me the key to navigating my way out of my current state.

"*We can complete this challenge together, I promise. We've done it before,*" she said, and she's right. We will and we have. I know that. I'm safe now that I've found her and this, and like all the other challenges I've ever faced in my life, this too will pass.

That's what I need to overcome this task from Hermes.

"Ella, we're so silly," Poppy claims through nervous laughter. "I just realized that you're being protected by the Eye of Horus, and it would protect me, too. I can take my headphones off!"

"No," I sign back to her quickly, as fresh determination replaces panic. "I need you to let go of me and go to the others. Stop them from going in the water. Take Maisie. Don't take your headphones off."

"I understand," she tells me. "What are you going to do?"

"I'm going to listen," I reply in sign.

She hesitates. "What? Ella, did I understand you right? Did you say you're going to 'listen'? Listen to who?"

"I'll explain later. Go now before it's too late," I sign in response.

"All right, I will," she says reluctantly. "I'm going to trust you."

Poppy squeezes my hands and then gets to her feet. She instructs Maisie to come with her and I hear her steadying herself by holding on to the side as she makes her way to the back of the boat with Maisie at her heels.

Channelling the calm bravery that Poppy has displayed, I take another deep breath. Everything will be OK. We have a plan now. My brain is no longer clouded with panic. My heart isn't beating out of control and I have a handle on my breathing. My mind isn't racing with worry or fear. I ground myself by focusing on my senses.

For the first time since I heard their song, I listen to what the sirens are saying.

CHAPTER TWENTY

"Do you believe things are meant to be?
For I believe you were meant to come
        to me.
You have travelled so far, you're tired
        and cold,
Come closer, come rest; have someone
        to hold.

My song will guide you, my words will
        soothe,
You've sailed in rough waters, jump into
        the smooth.
Away from the silence of sunrise you steer,
Closer, that's it, to where music rings clear.

The rays of the sun shall not dull my voice,
Come in or go back, you have your choice.
But do you believe things are meant to be?
For I believe you were meant to come
    to me."

It's the same three verses over and over. Something strikes me as odd about it, but I can't work out what it is.

"Come on, Ella, listen," I encourage myself out loud, as I get to my feet.

And just when I need a boost of hope, I get one from Poppy as I hear her yelling over their singing: "Ella, if you can hear me then I'm holding on to Finn and River! Maisie is pulling back Andrew!"

"Thank goodness," I whisper, pressing my hand against my heart.

"And to add as a sidenote," Poppy continues, "Maisie is pulling Andrew back by his trousers and it looks hilarious. They could tear at any moment and I'd see his pants! I know this is a serious situation, but just in case you needed some comic relief."

A bubble of laughter rises up my throat and escapes before I can stop it. It helps. Something lifts as I giggle, and I regret ever snapping at Poppy for not taking things seriously or for doing things her way. When this is over, I will tell her to *always* do things her way.

Still smiling, I listen again to the sirens' eerie song.

"Do you believe things are meant to be?
For I believe you were meant to come
    to me.
You have travelled so far, you're tired
    and cold,
Come closer, come rest; have someone
    to hold.

My song will guide you, my words will
    soothe,
You've sailed in rough waters, jump into
    the smooth.
Away from the silence of sunrise you steer,
Closer, that's it, to where music rings clear.

The rays of the sun shall not dull my voice,
Come in or go back, you have your choice.
But do you believe things are meant to be?
For I believe you were meant to come
    to me."

The repetition of the mention of the sun. *That's* what's snagging.

"What has the sunrise got to do with anything?" I ask out loud, pretending Poppy can hear me so I don't feel alone in this, frowning so hard in concentration my head aches. "Sirens live in the sea! And since when has sunrise been silent. It doesn't make any se—" I pause, inhaling sharply. "Wait a second – *'Away from the silence of sunrise you steer; Closer, that's it, to where music rings clear'* – are they saying that their music can't be heard by the sunrise? And then, *'The rays of the sun shall not dull my voice'*. Yes, that's it!"

The boat jolts and I hear a yelp from Poppy.

"OK, they're getting harder to hold on to, Ella!" she cries out. "So any time you want to beat Hermes's stupid challenge, that would be great. No offence, Hermes," she adds quickly, "don't come at me for calling your challenges 'stupid'. We've been through enough."

I feel my way to the helm, grabbing the wheel with one hand and reaching into my bag for the compass with the other.

"If the direction towards sunrise is where it's silent and where rays dull these voices, then that's where we want to steer," I declare to myself, feeling for the ball bearings. "And the sun rises in the east."

Guided by the compass, I spin the wheel, turning the boat round and heading in the opposite direction of where we were drifting.

"Come on," I say through gritted teeth as I find the throttle and push it forward.

The boat speeds up as we head east and the song gets quieter and quieter, until...

"It's gone," I whisper, scared to say it out loud in case I'm wrong. "I can't hear any music. The sirens have gone!"

Maisie barks loudly in celebration.

"Ella? Ella, are you driving the boat?" I hear Finn call out.

"Yeah!" I reply, laughing and pulling the throttle back to a slow speed. "I'm guessing the fog has lifted then. Andrew, are you there, because I could do with some help."

"I'm here!" he says, and I hear him clambering across the boat to get to me before I step aside to let him take over the helm. "What's going on? My head ... I'm so confused. I feel like I was sleepwalking!"

"You were, sort of," Poppy says, and she takes my hand to guide me back to my seat where Maisie greets me with slobbery licks across the face.

"What happened?" River asks, and there's a thud as he sits down nearby. "Did we fall asleep? I thought it was meant to be a short crossing."

"Someone was singing a lullaby," Finn says, sounding bewildered.

"Not someone, some *thing*," Poppy corrects. "And there were a few of them."

"A choir of them," I add.

"A choir of what?" he asks.

"Sirens," Poppy and I say in unison.

"*Sirens?*" River and Finn reply in chorus.

"As in the mythological creatures who sing songs to lure people into the water with fatal consequences?" Finn checks nervously. "*Those* sirens?"

"Yes," Poppy confirms. "It turns out that they caused a little bit of –" she pauses to create suspense before concluding – "panic."

"The next challenge from Hermes," Finn realizes straight away. "How did you overcome it, Ella? What did you do?"

"Actually, it was Poppy who saved the day. Without her, I wouldn't have made it through that challenge." I reach for her hand and squeeze it. "I'm so glad you're here."

"I'm glad I'm here, too," she says softly, and my eyes well up again.

"Hang on a minute," Andrew says, interrupting our moment. "Why are my trousers ripped at my bottom?!"

Poppy and I erupt into a fit of giggles.

CHAPTER TWENTY-ONE

Having steered us back on course, Andrew announces that we should be at Kisimul Castle any minute, but I can tell something is wrong because he begins to mutter under his breath in confusion.

"This isn't Kisimul Castle," Poppy states. "We visited it on our family holiday, and unless someone has taken a wrecking ball to the place since then, this is *not* the same castle."

"What do you mean?" I ask, putting Maisie's harness on and standing up.

"You remember, it was like a fortress, right? A medieval castle with big stone walls. I get that it was ancient and everything, but it was still standing," Poppy says. "This looks like a pile of ruins. It looks like it's been destroyed."

"She's right," Andrew whispers, horrified. "I don't understand! How has this happened? Who has done this? The fog may have obscured our sight of the castle, but we would have heard the walls crumble and fall. We would have heard if this…"

He trails off with a helpless whimper.

"I don't think this is real, Andrew," I say in an attempt to comfort him. "This is probably another of Hermes's tricks. You can't trust anything."

"Are you sure?" he asks breathlessly.

"As you say, you would have heard someone knocking down a castle. Everything we face on this journey is set up by Hermes to put us off the quest."

"To put *you* off the quest," River corrects gently. "The journey is designed personally to you, isn't it, Ella?"

I swallow the lump building in my throat. "Yes, it is."

"But I don't understand," Poppy sighs. "Why would Kisimul Castle be in ruins? Why would that make you want to turn back? Were you *that* scared of this castle? I guess parts of it were a little creepy."

Shaking my head, I get out Hermes's map. "It wasn't the castle I was scared of. It was what I was feeling when I climbed the tower with you and we stood at the top of it."

"What was that?" she asks curiously.

"That my whole life was about to crumble. So, it makes sense that Hermes would reduce it to ruins now. As River pointed out, he's making it personal."

No one says anything. I've maybe been a bit too blunt in my explanation, but there's no point in hiding the truth at this stage. They deserve to know why we're here.

"We came to Barra after that hospital appointment, the one where you got your diagnosis," Poppy says hoarsely, as though starting to understand. "It was meant to cheer you up, but…"

"It brought home the realities of what was going to happen," I finish for her when she trails off. "Barra was the most beautiful, magical place I'd ever seen. And I knew that I wouldn't ever be able to see it again."

Fighting back tears, I soon feel Poppy's warm hand gently take mine.

"That must have been terrifying," she says.

I give a sharp nod. I don't trust myself to speak.

"But you know now that you don't need to see Barra to experience its beauty," she says gently.

"You don't need to see a place to sense its magic and history."

Breaking into a smile, I allow a tear to fall before Poppy reaches up to wipe it away. "Yes, I know that now. But I didn't know that then. It was like all hope had been swallowed up. I was so scared of what I'd lose."

"And you had no idea of who you'd become," Poppy adds. "Ella, you don't need to be afraid any more. You know your strength. You know the *fire* inside of you. The fears you had then, you've already faced them. So whatever comes next, you know you've got that in the bag, too, right?"

I laugh weakly. "Yeah, I guess you're right."

"I *know* I'm right. I usually am."

"Not sure I agree with that, but –" I offer a sincere and grateful smile – "thanks, Poppy."

"Anytime," she says, squeezing my hand.

The boat knocks against the jetty as Andrew moors it. He leads the way off the boat, helping Maisie and me to get on dry land safely. While the others follow, I get the map out and wait for it to show me where we're supposed to go from here.

"There's another message coming up on the map," I announce to the group as raised Braille appears beneath my fingers.

"What does it say this time?" Poppy asks nervously, coming to stand next to me.

"What is that parchment?" Andrew asks in awe. "Those ink dots on it are changing!"

"It's a moving tactile map," Finn explains to him. "It speaks directly to Ella."

"You lot get more and more interesting," Andrew notes.

"Read it out to us," River says, coming to stand on my other side.

"OK." I clear my throat and begin to read the lines of the poem as they appear:

> "In the clutches of Panic, we stumble
>   and fall,
> A suffocating horror that comes to us all.
> We lose who we are in such loneliness and
>   fright,
> Yet, beyond heavy fog remains blue sky
>   and light.
>
> Panic seems never-ending, a paralysing
>   surge,
> But from the depths of a spiral, hidden
>   strength can emerge.

Within you, shield-seeker, is a
valiant glow,
For to give help is brave, to accept it
more so.

One step closer to the treasure, what now
can lie ahead?
I Fear you will be better off turning back
instead.
Nothing left to do but wish you well on
your endeavour,
For this, my friend, you'll need courage
more than ever."

As I finish reading it, the Braille slips away and raised lines appear on the map in its place, twisting and turning to form a symbol.

"It's a shield," I tell everyone, tracing the outline. "It must be here."

"We're close then," Finn remarks. "Just Fear and Fate to go."

"There's carvings on these stones that surround the path down towards the ruins!" River says suddenly, and I hear him move away to get a closer look. "Whoa, *loads* of carvings. They're everywhere."

"Who has done this to our castle?" Andrew rages, stomping off to inspect it himself.

"The map is changing again. It's forming another symbol," I say.

"What is that?" River wonders out loud, and I hear the crunch of his footsteps as he makes his way over heavy stones and rock. "Drawings of … uh …. oh."

"What are they?" Poppy calls out.

"Snakes," River answers. "Someone's carved snakes into the castle stones."

"*Snakes?*" Poppy shudders. "OK, you win, Hermes, I'm officially full of fear."

"Oooh, what kind of snakes?" Finn asks excitedly, and I hear him scurry over to River. "Hm. I don't recognize this particular species. Maybe whoever carved these into the stone was going for a generic snake. They're long with a triangular head and some kind of patterns along their scales. They look a bit like vipers."

"I think they were illustrating specific snakes that belong to someone," I inform him, as the symbol completes beneath my touch.

"Who?" Poppy asks, disgusted.

"A gorgon."

River gasps. "Are … are you sure?"

"I'm sure. The map is showing me some kind of monster with snakes for hair." I get out the compass and read what it's telling me. "I need to go straight ahead according to this. Does that make sense?"

"Straight ahead is down a path that takes us into the ruins, so yeah," Poppy answers.

"Not us," I say firmly, turning to face her. "Just me."

"*What?*" Poppy balks.

"You're not going in there alone," Finn insists, his voice closer as he rejoins us. "Ella, I think the map is leading you into Medusa's lair. She's probably the one guarding the shield."

"Definitely ticks a lot of fear boxes," River mutters, following Finn back.

"Medusa isn't the only gorgon in Greek mythology," Finn continues matter-of-factly. "There are also her sisters, Stheno and Euryale. If anything, they're more threatening than Medusa as they're immortal, whereas she was born mortal so could be defeated."

"Oh, that's good to know," Poppy says with heavy sarcasm. "How comforting you are in a crisis, Finn."

"Hopefully it'll just be Medusa in there, rather than all three of them," he adds quietly. "It makes more sense for it to be her guarding the shield. It's her story that we all know – you hear gorgon, you think Medusa, am I right?"

He attempts a laugh, but no one joins in. He turns his laugh into a cough.

"Anyway," he says, becoming serious again, "as there is a gorgon depiction on the shield itself, she probably sees it as her right to keep it as a treasure."

"There's a gorgon on the shield?" Poppy sighs. "Guess there's no chance we're wrong about one being in there among the ruins then. OK, how do we go about taking down a gorgon? Finn, any tips?"

Before he can answer, I jump in: "You're not coming in with me."

"We've already told you, you're not doing this alone," Finn says wearily.

"I have to. How does Medusa defeat her enemies, Finn? They look her in the eye and they turn to stone. I won't be able to do that, so I'll be safe."

Finn snorts. "You think that's all Medusa can do? Ella, she's capable of a lot more than simply waiting for someone to look her in the eye. There are stories about her being able to create illusions, manipulate objects, even fly with her wings. Not to mention the many, *many* venomous snakes on her head."

"But—"

"No 'buts'," Poppy interjects stubbornly. "We've come this far. We're in it together until the end. You heard what that poem from Hermes said – asking for and accepting help takes guts. We're offering our help, Ella, you need to be brave enough to accept it."

Maisie barks loudly.

"Exactly, Maisie, I agree," Finn adds. "Remember what River reminded us after we walked round and round in circles? We're a team. We don't abandon each other, no matter how hard it gets."

River sniffs. I give a wobbly smile, grateful but terrified.

"All right, we'll go in together," I say, relenting. "But if we're doing this, then we have to take precautions. You need to keep your eyes closed or on the ground and keep a hand on the shoulder of the person in front of you. Maisie and I will guide us. No matter what you hear, don't look up, or glance at anything. She'll try to tempt you to."

"Got it. Avoid taking a peek at the gorgon," Poppy says. "No one is turning to stone."

"And Andrew, you stay here by the boat," I instruct.

He doesn't respond.

"Hey, where is Andrew?" Poppy asks, sounding

bewildered. "I thought he was up ahead with you two when you were studying the snakes."

"So did I," Finn says slowly.

"He's not behind us?" I check with them. "Did he get back on the boat?"

"No, he's nowhere," River says. "He wouldn't have… No, he can't have done that. Surely not."

"Done what?" I ask urgently.

"Walked ahead of us into the gorgon's lair," River says timidly. "He did seem interested in what had happened to the castle."

"No," Poppy says, "there's no way that—"

"Hey, you have all got to come in here!" Andrew's voice calls out excitedly from inside the ruins. "Straight down the path and through the arch, it's like a cave of wonders in here! There're weapons lining the cave wall!"

"Andrew!" I shout at the top of my lungs. "You have to get out of there!"

"There's a huge mound of treasure in here," he replies in wonder, ignoring my desperate plea. "So much gold and… Wait, what is that? Aye, it's a shield! It's *magnificent*. It's silver and glowing. The detail on this thing is unbelievable. I'll carry it to you."

"Andrew, leave it and *run*!"

"It's nae bother, I can bring it out to you if you…"

There's a faint hissing sound that echoes through the ruins. Andrew screams just before we hear a heavy cracking, grinding sound of stone fixing into place before a final solid *thud*. And then silence.

"*No*," Poppy whispers.

I steel myself. "Last chance to stay here while I go in alone."

For a moment, no one replies, but then I feel Poppy's hand grip my shoulder. There are footsteps as the others fall in line behind her.

"We're ready, Ella," Poppy tells me.

"Whatever you do, don't look up," I remind them one last time before taking a deep breath and trying not to let my voice tremble as I give my instruction. "Maisie, forward."

A rumble of thunder roars through the sky above us as we walk into Medusa's lair.

CHAPTER TWENTY-TWO

Slowly and carefully, Maisie leads us down the path deep into the ruins.

We're all pretending to be braver than we feel. Poppy's hand is trembling on my shoulder, and I can hear Finn and River's shaky breathing behind her, and when my shoe kicks a pebble that scatters away and hits a rock, I jump at the noise, my heart pounding against my chest. A hissing sound brings us to an abrupt halt.

Maisie emits a low, warning growl.

"Ah, more guests have arrived," comes a woman's voice so chilling it makes the hairs on my arms stand on end. "Lucky me."

"Who are you?" I ask.

"You know who I am," she replies.

I gulp. "Medusa."

A chorus of snakes hissing echoes around the ruins. Poppy's nails dig into my shoulder. Medusa chuckles, as though amused.

"That's right," she says. "And who are you?"

"Ella Jones," I say, the wobble in my voice giving away my nerves.

She takes a moment before she speaks, and I get the feeling I'm being studied.

"And what do you want with me, Ella Jones?"

"You … you have something I need."

"Is that so?"

"The Shield of Hercules."

"Ah." I hear her take a couple of steps in our direction. My legs are shaking. "That's a precious item. I won't let you take it from me."

"You might not have a choice."

She hisses with laughter, her snakes all joining in. "Such courage in someone so young. Or might I be mistaking courage for stupidity? Arrogance, perhaps. It's yet to be determined."

"Tell me what I have to do to win the shield from you," I demand.

"Do you think you have what it takes to defeat me?" she asks, fascinated. "So many have failed before you. Like your friend here. He looks good in stone. Another statue to add to my collection. A local, was he?"

"I won't let Andrew stay like that," I tell her, balling my hand into a fist. "When we beat you, we'll make you turn him back."

"No one can make me do anything," she spits venomously, her snakes hissing and snapping, before she softens her voice again. "But how interesting that you brought friends with you. No one else has. Is it sweet or is it selfish on your part, to lead your loved ones into perilous danger? Either way, I get more stone statues to add to my collection, so I'm extremely grateful."

"It won't work, Medusa," I tell her. "You can't make me any more afraid."

"Oh, but I can, Ella Jones," she says, her icy voice sending rolls of shivers down my spine. "Everyone walks in here pretending they're not afraid, but I can *smell the fear.*"

I don't say anything, my jaw tensing as I try to hold my nerve.

"You may choose your weapon," she continues. "The wall to your right has a selection: swords, bows and arrows, spears. They were gifts to me from all the challengers who have come before you..." She hesitates. "I don't think they intended them to be gifts when they came here carrying them, but none of them have any need for them now. You may select whichever one you want and then you can challenge me. I will see what you're made of."

I frown. "You're offering me a weapon to fight you? This is a trap."

"You think so low of me that you believe I wouldn't make this a fair fight? My child, there would be no fun in that. I'm giving you a chance."

"It sounds more like you're giving me a death sentence."

Another chorus of hisses echoes before she sneers, "Then at least go down fighting. And choose your weapon wisely, Ella. Fear cannot be defeated easily."

My heart is racing. I lift my hand to push my hair away from my face, whisps of it sticking to the sweat on my brow.

"It's OK, Ella," Poppy says confidently, and I will for her courage to transfer to me. "I'm thinking you go for the bows and arrows and let each of us have a turn. You know I have good aim. One of us is bound to hit the target!"

"What if we don't and then we run out of arrows?" Finn says in a hushed voice behind her. "All Ella would be left to fight with is a useless bow."

"I … I can't fight," I admit quietly, but I'm not sure anyone hears.

"Go for a sword," Finn encourages. "It's a trusty weapon and a classic. If you're up against a gorgon, everyone knows you swipe at it with a sword."

"Why are these weapons so outdated?" River remarks from the back. "Not one piece of technology in this cave. Everything is *ancient*."

"That's probably because Medusa is from ancient mythology," Finn reminds him.

River snorts. "What, so no one has taken her on since then? She must have been bored out of her skull lurking here for centuries, waiting for—"

"QUIET!" Medusa roars, her snakes hissing furiously on her behalf.

We fall into terrified silence.

"You are running out of time," she informs me. "Choose your weapon and give it your best shot. And once I'm done with you, don't worry –" she chuckles evilly – "you won't be alone in your new stone form. Your little friends will join you after."

"Medusa—" I begin.

"*Choose your weapon*," she cries, her snakes hissing threateningly.

"No."

Poppy gasps. Medusa's snakes fall silent.

"No?" she repeats, surprised.

"No," I confirm, shaking my head to emphasize my point. "I don't want a weapon."

"Ella, what are you doing?" Finn squeaks.

"This is not good," River groans.

I hear footsteps as Medusa takes a few steps closer to me, but Maisie growls again and she stops where she is.

"Do you think that just because you can't see me, you shouldn't be afraid of me?" Medusa asks.

"No, I *am* afraid," I admit, swallowing as my mouth turns dry. "I meant it earlier when I said you can't make me any more afraid. You thought I meant to tell you I wasn't scared at all, but that's not it. I was saying you can't make me more afraid than I already am. Because –" I exhale and give a shrug – "I'm completely terrified."

Medusa doesn't say anything.

"Ella, are you sure this is a good idea?" Poppy whispers. "The swords are right *there*."

"Choosing a weapon isn't going to help anything," I

state. "I don't believe you overcome fear by pretending you don't have it and then running at the cause of it by swinging a sword or piercing it with an arrow."

"You admit that you're afraid," Medusa muses.

"Yes. This isn't the first time I've faced fear like this."

"Oh?" she prompts, intrigued.

"I felt it here on this very island some years ago," I tell her. "That's why Hermes brought me to Barra; that's why we're here. It was here that I knew there would come a time when I would never see a beautiful view like the ones of Barra again. I wouldn't be able to see my parents' faces and Poppy's face. I wouldn't be able to look in the mirror again and see *me*. I thought I was going to lose who I was, and who I thought I was going to grow up to be. I felt lost and helpless and alone. I lost all hope. So, yes, I have known fear – I have been to the darkest point in my mind."

"And how did you overcome that fear?" Medusa asks, her snakes giving a low hiss.

"I'm not sure I ever did," I admit. "I cried a lot. I got angry about why it was happening to me and not someone else. It's like when Ailynn told us about the shield. I thought, 'Why does it have to be me who goes?' And even when we walked into the ruins

259

of this castle knowing you were here inside, I was thinking, 'Why is it us who are here? Why can't it be someone else?'"

"An interesting question," Medusa says.

"Not one I can answer," I admit. "I can't answer it today, and I couldn't answer it when I was told I was going to lose my sight. Instead, all I can do is accept that it's OK to be afraid. It's OK to cry and fall down sometimes. What's important is you get back up."

Maisie lifts her head to lick my hand. Poppy squeezes my shoulder.

I'm never alone.

"I need that shield to make sure it doesn't fall into the hands of someone who is going to use it for all the wrong reasons," I continue. "So I have to hope that there's some other way of getting it from you without having to pick up a weapon and fight you for it."

"*Hope*," Medusa repeats, her tone sneering. "That's all you bring to the mighty Medusa. Nothing but weak, frail hope."

"Hope isn't weak or frail, it's the strongest armour I know," I say, frowning. "The moments in my life when I've lost hope have been the most fearful. Hope is what has got all of us this far. We couldn't have walked in here without it."

"And now, Ella Jones, it is hope that brings you to the end."

No.

As the snakes' hissing fills the air, I brace myself for an attack, but instead I feel a gust of wind swirl around me, whipping my hair across my face, almost knocking me off my feet. I gasp, trying to keep my balance in the centre of a tornado. Then everything goes still, silent and calm. I feel a warm glow on my skin. I have no idea what's going on but I somehow know that I am safe here.

"The shield is yours."

I jump at Medusa speaking. Her voice is all around me now, not just coming from one specific place, but as though she is everywhere all at once.

"Wh-what?" I stammer in reply, realizing that Maisie's harness is no longer in my grip and I can't feel Poppy's hand on my shoulder. I'm all alone. "Where am I?"

"You are in my cave still. You haven't left."

"It feels like I have. Where's Maisie? Where are my sister and friends?"

"They are with you. If they dare to open their eyes, they'll be witnessing a magical spectacle as the Shield of Hercules offers its power and allegiance to you."

"What does that mean?" I ask, my mind trying to make sense of it all.

"The shield belongs to you now, Ella Jones. Trust it. It will take you to where you need to go. You have been a worthy opponent," Medusa says, her voice fading.

"I don't understand!"

"You chose your weapon wisely," she concludes, her voice barely audible, becoming lost in a chorus of hisses before it falls completely silent.

"Wait! What is—"

Before I can finish my question, my words are caught in a spiralling breeze and I feel Maisie's harness once more in my hand.

"Ella! Ella, are you OK?" Poppy asks, her grasp returning to my shoulder. "An energy force knocked me back and I lost hold of you, and I didn't want to look up, but it was like the whole cave was shrouded in this swirling silver, glittering mist! It was beautiful."

Still too confused to speak, I hear a loud clattering sound as a heavy object scatters across the floor and knocks into my shoes. There's a brief scraping sound as Maisie nudges it forward curiously with her nose, sniffing and inspecting it.

I crouch down, feeling for the object, running my hands over its surface.

"It's the Shield of Hercules," I tell the others. "It's ours."

"What?" Finn gasps. "How?"

"Medusa told me the shield belonged to me now; that I'd chosen my weapon wisely."

"I don't understand," Poppy says, kneeling down next to me. "So, is she gone?"

"I think so. Don't look up just in case," I instruct sternly. "It could be a trick."

"We won't," she promises.

"The Shield of Hercules," Finn whispers, bending down on my other side. "It's amazing. Ella, can you feel all the detail of the depictions?"

I nod, my fingers tracing the outlines. "Yes, there's a lot of stories on here."

"We did it," River croaks in disbelief. "*We actually did it.*"

"What happens now?" Poppy says.

"She said the shield will take us to where we need to go," I inform them.

"How does it do that?" River asks.

"I'm not entirely sure. Maybe Hermes will tell us," I say hopefully.

Reaching for the map in my pocket, I open it and lay it out on top of the shield as Braille appears across it. I read the poem to the others:

> "'Step into the shadows,' they say, 'if
>   you dare,
> For there lurks a monster with snakes in
>   her hair.
> No mercy, no questions, attack with no pause,
> Before she can strike with her fangs or her
>   claws,
>
> Or with one glance turn you there into
>   stone,
> Left cold and forgotten in her cave all
>   alone.'
> Yet if we approach with fear, rage
>   and hate,
> More merciless monsters I fear we create.
>
> When all feels lost and the end seems near,
> Hope is the weapon that can conquer Fear.
> A glittering star in the darkest of skies,
> We fall but, with hope, we believe we
>   can rise.

One very last thing that you need to know,
Put your hands on the shield and off you
     will go.
Over your journey, I have gladly presided,
But now it's by you that your Fate is
     decided."

CHAPTER TWENTY-THREE

I'm the last person to place my hands on the shield. Having instructed everyone else to kneel down round it and put their palms on the surface, I fold the map up to put it away and tell Maisie to step up on to the shield, too.

"What about Andrew?" Finn asks miserably.

"When all this is over, we'll work out a plan to save him," I assure him, the guilt tugging at my chest. "I'll speak to Ailynn, she'll know what to do."

"If you can hear us, Andrew, we're going to come back and save you," Finn says, raising his voice. "I promise."

"What do you think is going to happen when you put your hands on the shield, Ella?" Poppy asks.

I exhale a shaky breath. "Only one way to find out. Is everyone ready?"

They tell me that they are and Maisie sneezes.

"Good. OK, Shield of Hercules, time to take us to where we need to go."

Reaching down, I place my hands on top of the shield.

Suddenly, I lurch forward and tumble over but the ground beneath me has slipped away, so I don't hit anything. It's like I've been sucked into a tunnel and I'm falling down through it, until my knees knock against a surface and all is still again. Catching my breath, I find that I'm on some kind of cold, smooth flooring.

"Anyone else feel like they just got off a roller coaster?" Poppy whispers.

"My head is still spinning," River comments.

"I think I might be sick," Finn murmurs.

"Where are we?" I ask quietly, taking my hands off the shield and getting to my feet.

We're no longer in Medusa's cave or a medieval castle or any kind of ancient ruins, I know that much. It smells clean and new in here, like a freshly cleaned hotel room, studio or modern office – from the smooth, squeaky floor beneath my trainers, I'd guess it's some kind of dance studio or maybe a smart office, but it's too quiet for that. I can't hear any people or computers or phones. When anyone speaks, their voice echoes, so I know whatever room we're in, it's big.

"We're in a huge, circular room surrounded by glass from ceiling to floor," Poppy tells me, as I hear her scrambling to her feet. "Hang on, let me look out the... *Whoa.*"

"What is it?"

"We're high up," she says, astounded. "Like, *really* high up. I can see out across the whole city. This must be some kind of London skyscraper and we're on the top floor! Yep, this is definitely the penthouse of this building."

"The shield has brought us to London?" I say, putting my hands on my hips.

"There's a desk over here with a computer," Finn says, his shoes squeaking across the floor as he goes to check it out. "Let me move the mouse and see if the screensaver gives a clue as to who it belongs to."

"You know, this place seems kind of familiar," Poppy says slowly.

"Have you been here before?" I ask.

"No, I don't think so. I can't put my finger on it, but I feel like—"

"You recognize it," Finn finishes for her, his voice croaky. "I know why you would. The logo on the screensaver has told me exactly where we are. We're in Croft Tower!"

I freeze, my breath catching. "Wh-what?"

"Yes, that's it!" Poppy exclaims. "It's Everett Croft's building. We've walked past it so many times and seen it on TV. No wonder it felt familiar."

"Why would the shield bring us here?" Finn asks, aghast.

"It was supposed to take us to where we needed to go," I whisper, pressing my hand against my forehead as my brain tries to make sense of it all. "I thought it would take us somewhere safe, to someone who could help us. Why would it bring us *here*?"

"This is Everett Croft's office," Finn notes. "There's a gold desk plate here reading 'Everett Croft, CEO'. It makes sense that he'd be in the penthouse."

"From the lair of one monster, straight to the lair of another," Poppy mutters.

Maisie whines loudly, staying next to the shield as though knowing to guard it.

"River, are you OK?" Finn asks, sounding concerned. "You've gone pale."

"I'm fine," River answers quickly.

"It's OK if you're still feeling queasy from that trip with the shield from Medusa's lair," Poppy says kindly. "I don't feel so great myself. You could sit down over at the desk."

"No, it's … I'm fine."

"I still don't understand why the shield would bring us here," Finn wonders aloud.

"At least no one is here," Poppy says, coming over to me. "But if Everett Croft comes to his office any time soon, he'll take that shield off you, no question."

"It wouldn't matter, it's incomplete without the Eye of Horus," I remind her. "As long as I've got the pendant, the power of the shield will only work for me. We need to complete the shield now before anyone finds us here. If the shield is complete and loyal to me, then Homados can't use it. He can't take it from me and there's no chance I'll hand it over."

"There's a lift over here, I'll guard it and make sure no one is coming," Poppy offers. "Finn, search the desk for clues as to why the shield would bring us here. There's got to be a reason."

"I'm looking," he says, as I hear objects being slid and rattled across the desk. "So far there's nothing that explains this situation."

"River, help me with the shield," I instruct,

kneeling back down in front of it and fiddling with the clasp of the delicate chain round my neck. "You said there's a space for the pendant in the centre of it?"

"Yes, it's a hollowed-out shape of an eye right in the middle, so it's obvious. Do you need me to help you find it?"

"No, it's OK," I say, as I carefully take off the pendant. "Here, hold this. Can you take the chain off? I'll find the space it's meant to go."

Using both hands, I feel across the raised detailed depictions decorating the surface of the shield until I find the smooth socket the exact size and shape of the Eye of Horus carved out in the centre of the shield just as River said.

"Found it," I declare, holding out my hand. "OK, give me the pendant."

My palm remains empty.

"River?" I prompt, wiggling my fingers. "You can give it back now."

Still, nothing.

"River, what are you doing?" Finn asks, taking a pause in rummaging through Everett Croft's desk. "Now is not the time to study the pendant."

"Yeah, we know it's pretty, but Ella needs to put

it in the shield," Poppy adds with a nervous chuckle. When he doesn't respond, she says, "River? *River!*"

I can tell from her voice that something is wrong.

"I'm so sorry," River whispers.

"Why are you sorry? What's going on? River, give me back the Eye of Horus," I demand desperately.

Maisie starts barking wildly, backing up as she stands purposefully between me and whatever it is that has put her on high alert. I hear the swishing sound of a door opening automatically from the opposite side of the room to where Poppy is standing by the lift. Poppy gasps, Finn yelps in fear and even River emits a nervous whimper. Two pairs of footsteps enter the room. One light, the other solid and heavy. Too heavy to be human. I can sense a change in the room's atmosphere at their entrance. The temperature seems to drop, and the air feels charged. I'm covered in goosebumps and I have no idea who it is yet.

"Ella Jones, we meet again," Everett Croft says through a menacing cackle. "Allow me to introduce you to my new friend. This is Homados."

Now I understand their reaction. We're in the presence of a god.

Homados doesn't say anything, but he doesn't need to. His presence is enough to strike fear into anyone in his vicinity. I can feel power and fury radiating from him.

"Poppy, Finn, *hide*!" I cry out in a desperate attempt to protect them, but Everett Croft barks with laughter. It's too late for that.

Maisie snarls and growls at him menacingly, but I put a hand on her back and she stops, snorting indignantly, reluctant to back down. I appreciate her guarding us, but I'd rather she didn't threaten the god of tumult and battle noise.

"There's nowhere for you to hide now," Everett says smugly. "Even if my office weren't designed to the most excellent of minimalist tastes, there's nothing that could hide you well enough. I'm afraid your little quest ends here, Ella Jones. A stroke of luck that you've brought the shield to us with very little intervention from myself, I must say. I had planned on instructing our pilot to bring you straight back from Barra to London, and then I'd have a convoy waiting for you at the airport, but here you are in my office!" He claps his hands and rubs them together. "Splendid."

"How did you know we were in Barra?" I stammer, bewildered.

"Oh, I've known *everything*, Ella, right from the

start," he tells me, sounding amused at my ignorance and relishing in the big surprise. "I know how worried you were about these bouts of unbearable noise. I know you scampered along to your friend at that grubby museum to ask her advice. I know how you robbed the pathetic Lord Almond to retrieve the map and compass which would only work for you with the Eye of Horus, and that you made your way to Scotland. I know you managed to hitch a lift to Barra and then you muddled your way through tasks to earn the Shield of Hercules."

"You've been following us!" Poppy accuses, her voice wobbling a little and betraying her fear. I know she's not afraid of Everett Croft, but Homados must be as imposing as I suspect, and his continued silence is eerily intimidating.

Everett chortles. "I didn't have to, Poppy. Who do you think set you on this course in the first place? It's been my plan all along and you've played your parts marvellously."

"I don't understand," I croak.

"It doesn't surprise me that you're slow on the uptake," he sighs, tutting loudly. "That's your problem, Ella, you're too *trusting* in human nature. You want to believe the good in people and that's why you'll never be as successful as me. I've always known that humans are selfish and greedy and unbelievably gullible. People will believe whatever you tell them. That's how I've risen to the top –" he pauses – "*Literally*. We could not be any higher in the city right now. It's a spectacular view, isn't it?"

"I think we have different ideas about what success is," I manage to say more confidently than I feel. "I'd rather be surrounded by loving family and friends than be stuck up here alone in a cold empty office, no matter how good the view is."

"But that's where you're wrong!" he trills, ecstatic with joy. "I'm not alone."

"You think Homados cares about you?" Finn says nervously. "If you know anything about mythology like you claim you do, you'd know that gods will happily use humans to do their bidding and then cast them aside when they've gained the power they want."

"Firstly, Homados and I have a deal," Everett snaps, bristling at Finn's remark, before he relaxes his tone to continue. "Secondly, it wasn't him to who I was referring when I said I wasn't alone. You think one of the differences between us is that I don't have a loving, loyal family like yours, Ella, but I do. You should know this."

"What are you talking about?" I ask.

"When Homados revealed his ambitions to me, I knew I could help him get what he wanted," Everett begins, taking another step towards me. Maisie emits a low growl. "To complete the Shield of Hercules – a treasure that would help to give him ultimate power over the world and his fellow gods – he needed the Eye of Horus, the very item that would make the map and compass work to lead the way to the shield. He knew Lugh had got rid of it."

"He didn't get rid of it," Poppy counters bitterly. "He *gave* it to Ella to protect her."

Everett clicks his fingers, the loud snap making me jump. "Exactly. The Eye of Horus doesn't work for its beholder unless it's given willingly, and the Shield of Hercules doesn't work without the Eye of Horus, nor do Hermes's map and compass. Quite the pickle for Homados."

"You knew Ella would never give it to someone who wanted to use it for selfish gain and merciless power," Finn says with a hint of pride in his voice.

"Unfortunately, yes, I knew enough about you to know that," he admits. "But I also knew you well enough to know how easy it would be to get you to hand it over willingly. If you knew that Homados was after the shield, you would do all the work and go retrieve it for us. All I had to do was place someone close to you who could win your trust, someone who could earn your friendship. It was so easy in the end. You didn't question his friendship for a moment. You gave him the pendant without a second thought."

The truth hits me so hard, I feel winded.

"It's my pleasure to introduce you to my brilliant and loyal nephew who has played his role to perfection," Everett concludes. "River, please, take a bow."

CHAPTER TWENTY-FOUR

I don't believe it. I don't *want* to believe it.

"No," Finn says hoarsely. "No, you're lying!"

"He's a very good actor," Everett chuckles. "He fooled you all much easier than I expected. It was no trouble at all to enrol him in your school and he befriended you straight away. Even I was impressed."

"Ella, I'm so sorry," River says, and my blood chills.

"Everett Croft is your uncle?" Poppy says. "It can't be true."

Everett heaves a sigh. "You're all very slow today, of *course* it's true. Where do you think he got all his brilliant gadgets from? How do you think he paid for everything? Why would it be so easy for him to find a pilot to take you to Barra at the last minute? Because the pilot works for me! Success runs in the family. My sister – River's mother – has done well to develop her own tech company and when we bring our resources together, we're unstoppable." He coughs. "She doesn't know anything about this particular plan as of yet, but I'm sure she'd be delighted with River's involvement."

"I don't believe it," I say firmly, turning to River. "I don't believe it was a lie."

"Don't be so naive, Ella," Everett says tiredly. "Do you honestly think a kid you randomly meet at your school would be so quick to go along with your plan? Any other child would have run for the hills the moment you mentioned this being the work of a god."

"Ella, I had to," River says meekly.

"He forced you into this," I say.

"I didn't force him into anything!" Everett claims. "He was happy to be a part of it. He couldn't have leaped at the chance to befriend and betray you all quicker!"

"That's not … I didn't…" River searches for words, flustered. "You don't understand. My parents are never around, I never had any friends. No one has ever noticed me – except for Irving, and he's my butler. He's *paid* to notice me." River sniffs. "Then when Uncle Everett came over once, he noticed I was interested in the tech gadgets I'd been given and he ... he said I might amount to something after all. He was the one who taught me how important it is to become successful, to earn money and gain power. He said it was normal to feel alone. That it was better that way. He's the only one who believed I could *be* someone."

"He's used you," Poppy says bitterly.

"He's family," River points out. "The only family who has made me feel wanted and important. I wanted to feel like I belonged somewhere for the first—"

"Yes, yes, we're all very proud and so on and so forth," Everett interrupts dismissively. "Now, hand over that pendant. Come on, you need to hand it over willingly."

Nothing happens.

"River, *give me the Eye of Horus*," Everett orders in a strained voice.

"I think you mean he should give it to *me*," a deep, low, resonating voice says, a voice that makes me shudder.

"Oh, uh, yes of course, Homados!" Everett squeaks. "River, give the Eye of Horus to Homados. *Now.*"

But River is hesitating. I feel a glimmer of hope. The most powerful weapon we have.

"River, it's OK," I say, offering him a small smile. "I understand and I forgive you."

"*You do?*" Poppy hisses in surprise.

"Yeah, I do," I insist, continuing to address River. "I know what it's like to feel like you're stuck on the outside, to feel unnoticed on the sidelines. I know how it feels to want to belong. I can understand why you did what you did. But that doesn't mean things haven't changed, because they have."

"What are you talking about?" Everett says irritably. "River, ignore her and hand over the pendant at once!"

"You deserve more than an uncle who thinks your only value is to help him with his evil plans to take over the world and bring more pain and war to it," I tell River brazenly. "You deserve to know what an amazing friend you are. I don't care what Everett Croft says. As far as I'm concerned, you *are* my friend. I couldn't have done any of this without you."

"He was pretending the entire time. It was all a *lie*," Everett snaps at me.

"No, it wasn't," Finn cries, and I hear the squeak of his trainers as he moves from behind Everett's desk and comes to stand with me and Maisie. "Ella's right. It might have started out as an act, but we became true friends. River, you were there alongside us every step of the way, even when things got hard. You had our backs. Maybe at first it was for the wrong reasons, but I think you'd do the same for us now, wouldn't you?"

"I—"

Everett cuts off River, yelling, "We don't have time for this! River, remember who you work for … I mean, remember to who you are loyal. Think of the family name! Remember who you are."

"River knows exactly who he is, and it's got nothing to do with his family name," Poppy declares, coming to stand alongside us, too. "We all make mistakes but that's OK. We don't care about how this started, we care about what it's become. River, you're who you are because of what you do and the choices you make, not because of what your family name is. Like Finn said, you've been there for us during this quest, walking with us into Medusa's lair, helping us when we got a bit lost—"

"For goodness' sake! He had to help you when you were lost so you could find the shield that we needed," Everett bellows impatiently.

"That's not what I was talking about," Poppy says. "I meant when Ella and I were bickering and we forgot what was important, it was River who

284

reminded us that we were a team. And now it's our turn to remind him of that."

"River, they're trying to confuse you," Everett says. I can sense a tone of desperation which means River must look as though he's wavering. "Think about why you're in my office. The shield brought you all *here*. What can that mean? That it belongs to Homados and me! If it didn't, this would be the last place it would bring you!"

"You're wrong," I say.

"Excuse me?" Everett snaps.

"I said, you're *wrong*," I repeat louder this time. "I've been wondering why it would bring us here, but suddenly it makes sense. Hermes said it was me who had decided my own fate – the final challenge – and that the shield would take me where I needed to go. My fate was decided right from the beginning: I made the decision that I was going to stop you, Homados. And the shield has brought me here to face you so I can do just that."

"We don't run away from challenges, we face them," Finn says proudly.

"We accept when things go wrong and when we fall, we find the strength to get back up again and face them even stronger," Poppy adds.

There's a beat of silence before River whispers, "And we face them together."

I break into a wide smile.

"This pendant doesn't belong to me," River says, raising his voice.

"Finally!" Everett says, irritated.

"It belongs to Ella."

River steps forward, takes my hand, turns it so that my palm is facing upwards and then places the Eye of Horus into it, closing my fingers around the pendant and letting go.

"*No!*" Homados roars.

Any joy from River's action vanishes instantly as Homados's incensed cry pierces the air, making me stumble back in fright. I hold the pendant tight in my grasp.

"You dare to deny me what is mine?" Homados says in a frenzied, thunderous voice. "Listen to what you have done! Listen to the pain and fear you have caused!"

He begins to hiss a strange incantation in a language I don't understand.

There's no gradual build-up to the unbearable noise this time. The sound of battle comes screaming into the room, and while the pendant grows hot in my hand, everyone else collapses to the floor in agony.

"No! NO!" Everett yells, succumbing to the noise and his rage immediately. "You shall pay for this! All of you! River, you have betrayed me and you have betrayed your family! This is all your fault! The world will destroy itself because of you!"

Fixing the pendant quickly round my neck to free up my hands, I focus on staying calm as the noise escalates, testing the power of the Eye of Horus and making me wince.

"It's OK," I say urgently. "Poppy, Finn, River – try to listen to my voice. Fight what the noise is urging you to do. Find the sound of my voice within."

"They will never hear you," Homados says, and I shuffle backwards as I hear his heavy rumbling footsteps approach me.

He begins to laugh, that maniacal laugh I've heard before.

Maisie barks frantically, but I grab her collar and encourage her to back away from him. But Homados hasn't come striding over for us. He has come for the shield and has picked it up from the floor. I sense him towering over me, and I crouch next to Maisie with one hand on her back, feeling the vibrations of her intense growling.

"Your friends are suffering," Homados tells me

maliciously, as I hear the cries and whimpers of Poppy, Finn and River, while Everett continues to shout at anyone and anything. "They're doing their best to be strong and I admit they're faring better than some –" he pauses as Everett attempts to pick an argument with one of his windows – "but they won't last. Soon, they'll give in to the rage that's coursing through their veins as we speak. They'll argue with each other until they're enemies. That's how this will go, Ella Jones."

I grimace as I hear River beg for the noise to stop.

"If you give me the Eye of Horus, I will protect them. Under my rule, they will be safe. I promise," Homados says.

"I don't believe you," I cry. "You must have made that promise to Everett and listen to him now. He's not protected."

"He is weak. We both know that. You and your friends are stronger. I respect that."

"Then make this stop!" I plead. "Please!"

"You can make it stop, by giving me the pendant."

I shake my head. "No."

"Their eyes are shut from the pain, Ella. The noise in their head consumes and frightens them. They do not have what it takes to fight the evil inside of them. That's the beauty of my power over humans. I use their own rage against them. With a little nudge from me, they listen to what they really want and then they destroy themselves. They create their own battles, and then I step in to rule them all. They are weak and I am strong."

"My sister and my friends will find the strength to fight back."

As River yelps in pain, I don't care that Homados is looming over me, I begin to crawl across the floor in the direction of his voice.

"I'm here!" I tell them. "I'm right here! Listen to my voice. Find my voice!"

And then I feel a hand clasp my wrist. Poppy moves my hand over hers as, weak and tired, she uses tactile sign language to communicate: "*I found you.*"

CHAPTER TWENTY-FIVE

I clutch Poppy's hand gratefully. "Yes, you did! You did, I'm here! I'm always right here. Poppy, you have to help me find the others so the pendant can protect them, too."

As her strength starts to return thanks to the Eye of Horus, she shuffles forward on her knees and brings Finn's hand to mine. Gripping it tight as his pain begins to subside, he presses my hand against his cheek that's wet from tears.

"Thank you, Ella," he croaks.

"Where's River?" I ask, before Poppy manages to grab his hand and bring it into mine. I hold on to both of them tightly. "River, are you OK?"

He takes a moment to catch his breath. "How … how are you doing this? How are you making the noise fade away?"

"The Eye of Horus, remember. It protects me and those I love from the work of gods."

"But then if it's helping me, I really am…" He trails off, shaky and hesitant.

"You really are my friend," I tell him earnestly. "We meant what we said, River."

As River sobs, Maisie slips underneath my outstretched arm to nuzzle against my chest, and I rest my cheek on her fur.

No matter what happens now, at least we have each other.

"What are you going to do?" Homados interjects with a violent laugh. "Hold on to your friends forever? Is that your great plan? Love can do nothing. The world will crumble! Already the noise is doing its work. People all over your planet are fighting."

My mind is racing as I desperately try to think of a plan to stop him.

"Give me what I want, and I will stop this," he offers.

"You'll only stop it for now, but then you'll make it worse until everyone grows more and more unstable and there's actual battles, maybe even wars," I say, wincing as Everett picks up his computer and accuses it of harassing him with software updates before he smashes it on the floor. "I won't give you the Eye of Horus. You are not worthy of it!"

"You leave me no choice," Homados spits in a sinister voice. "You have stood in my way for too long. I will have to get rid of you altogether. You, your friends and your dog."

"Then the Eye of Horus will never work for you!" I point out, feeling sick as I hear his footsteps come closer and Maisie whines. "It has to be given willingly."

"I will work out a way. I am a *god*," he growls. "Goodbye, Ella Jones."

I duck my head into Maisie's fur as we all clutch each other's hands.

But as Homados roars with fury before delivering his final blow, the Eye of Horus grows hot, and a surge of power explodes from the pendant. The energy blasting from it is so forceful that I almost let go of everyone's hands, my hair flies back from my face and I hear Homados lose his balance and stumble backwards, dropping to the floor. The unbearable noise stops and I hear a new set of heavy footsteps, the floor vibrating from their force.

"Homados, I should have known it was you."

I recognize the voice immediately.

"Lugh!" I breathe, my heart leaping. "You're here!"

"The Eye of Horus called me to your aid," he says. "I'm only sorry I didn't come sooner. I was waylaid." His voice drops into a growl as he addresses Homados. "I take it that was your work."

"You didn't enjoy my gift?" Homados spits, as I hear him scramble to his feet.

"I'm not sure I'd describe a surprise visit from the Machai as a *gift*," Lugh says furiously.

"Oh? I thought you were overdue a catch-up with the daemons of battle," Homados replies. "You could do with a reminder of whose side you're on, Lugh. From what I can tell, you've gone a bit soft."

"Don't push me, Homados."

"It was humans who locked you up for millennia, yet it was a human to whom you gifted the Eye of Horus, one of the most precious items of the gods," Homados says venomously. "You *disgust* me."

"Ella Jones helped me to understand the importance of forgiveness and reminded me that people have an admirable capacity to change," he replies. "Not to mention, she saved me. I gave her that pendant because she was worthy to wear it, unlike you."

"When I have the shield and force humans under

my rule, I will make sure that you are punished for giving it away," Homados seethes.

"Hand that shield over," Lugh says calmly. "You know it is incomplete."

"It may not be all-powerful without the pendant, but it can still deflect attack, which means I might find it useful in what is to come."

"Why, what is to come?" Lugh asks.

Homados roars with fury, before I hear him charge at Lugh who grunts as he's tackled to the ground, the two of them falling with a thud so heavy it shakes the whole building. Lugh must have been holding his spear, but Homados knocks it away with the force of the shield, and I hear the spear clatter across the floor out of Lugh's reach. There's a loud clang as Homados strikes Lugh with the shield. Finn and River gasp with horror, but Poppy doesn't hesitate, jumping to her feet.

"Poppy!" I cry out as she runs in the direction of Everett's desk, behind which I have no doubt that Everett is cowering. I appeal to Finn: "What is she doing?"

"Uh, she's picked up the computer monitor from the floor and now she's running at Lugh and Homados," Finn narrates nervously. "And she's lifting the screen up behind her head as though she's going to thr—"

He's interrupted by Poppy's bloodcurdling battle cry. There's a *whoosh* of something big and heavy being hurled through the air, followed by a loud *smack* as the object comes into contact with someone's head.

"She … she just threw the monitor at Homados's head," Finn croaks.

"Did she hit her target?" I ask with a gulp, already knowing the answer.

"Yep."

"Is he angry?"

"Yep."

"Uh oh," I whisper.

"Take that, Homados!" Poppy shouts at the top of her lungs. "You want to pick on humans? Come on then, I'm wide open!"

"Poppy, what are you—"

My strangled question is cut off by Homados's thunderous growl as he pushes himself up and rounds on Poppy.

"OK, I'm going to run away now," I hear her say in a strangled voice, before she runs back towards us, the soft, hurried steps of her trainers followed by the heavy strides of a thunderous god.

"Watch out!" Finn yells, and I clasp a hand over my mouth, terrified of what's coming.

As Poppy trips and falls, landing in a heap in front of us, I throw myself over her and Maisie jumps up to stand between her and Homados. But we didn't need to, because I hear an "*Oof*" from Homados as Lugh leaps at him from behind, taking him down and knocking the shield out of his grasp.

It skitters away and I hear it knock against the glass wall.

"Maisie, fetch," I instruct in a low voice, and she sprints off before dragging it back across the floor to me. It's too heavy for her to pick up completely in her jaws.

"Good girl, Maisie," I whisper, taking it from her with one hand and using the other to unclasp my pendant. "You really are the *best* girl."

She gives my cheek a slobbery lick in agreement.

While the gods grapple with each other, I place the Eye of Horus in the middle of Hercules's shield. It slots in perfectly, and I feel the shield grow warm as the magic ripples out from the centre to every corner, my hands tingling as the power of the shield completes.

"Ella, quick!" Finn encourages in a hushed voice.

"Homados is standing over Lugh and he has his spear."

It's strange. Up until now, the shield has been heavy, but as I get to my feet and pick it up, I find it's light and easy to wield. River did remind us that the shield is loyal to its beholder once the Eye of Horus completes it. In this moment, the shield feels as though it was created for me.

"You really have gone soft, Lugh," Homados is saying victoriously. "I didn't want this, but if piercing you with your own spear is the only way to stop you, then so be it."

I hear the swish of the spear being pulled high back in the air over Homados's shoulder before he prepares to let it drop. I dive in front of Lugh, holding up the shield. As the spear touches the shield, a magical surge of power and energy bursts from the point of contact, sending Homados flying backwards through the air with a cry of surprise and shattering every glass panel around the room.

CHAPTER TWENTY-SIX

My hair whips across my face as the cold evening air whistles through the broken windows of Everett Croft's penthouse office. In the shocked silence that follows, broken only by the tinkling sound of pieces of glass still dropping to the floor, I slowly lower the shield.

"Ella! Ella, are you OK?" Poppy asks, rushing over to me and enveloping me in a hug. She pulls back to hold my face in her hands. "Ella, did he hurt you?"

"I'm fine," I assure her, breaking into a relieved smile. "Is Lugh OK?"

"Yes, thanks to you," Lugh says, and I hear him rise to his feet behind me. "Yet again, Ella Jones, I find myself in your debt. You saved my life."

"You saved ours by coming here, so count it even.

Where's Homados?" I ask, instinctively lifting the shield just in case.

Lugh strides across the room and stops, I assume to inspect the state of his fellow god.

"He's currently indisposed," he reports. "I imagine he'll wake up with a bad headache. That's what tends to happen when you attempt to challenge the unshakable powers of the Shield of Hercules."

"Is everyone all right?" I call out, as Maisie comes bounding over and I crouch down, dropping the shield on the floor to give her a big cuddle.

"We're fine!" Finn says as I straighten. "That was the most magical moment *ever*."

"It was *incredible*," Poppy gushes, passing me Maisie's harness which I slot over her head. Being so high up with all the windows broken, I like the reassurance of Maisie at my side. "When the spear hit the shield, there was a huge burst of silver, glittering light that filled the room and lit up the sky. It knocked Homados all the way across the room, he did backwards somersaults through the air the entire way. Oh, and Maisie's jowls were flapping wildly in the wind, slobber spraying everywhere!"

I burst out laughing at her description, reaching down to pat Maisie's head.

"It took out every glass panel in Everett's office," Poppy continues. "It's a bit scary up here now with no walls. I think we should go down but I don't fancy using the lift."

"The door that Everett came through earlier, does that lead to the stairs?" I check.

Before Poppy can answer, I hear the door slam.

I frown. "What was that?"

Poppy gasps. "Everett Croft! He's gone!"

"He's trying to escape!" Finn cries.

"He won't get far." I grip Maisie's harness. "Come on, let's follow him downstairs."

"That's not where he'll be going," River says, falling into step with Maisie and me. "Don't go down, go up. We have to go to the roof!"

"What's on the roof?" Poppy asks, swinging open the door for us to hurry through.

"A helipad," he answers.

With Poppy leading the way up the stairs, the fastest of the group, Maisie guides me safely up another flight before we step out on to the roof of Croft Tower. I can hear the whirring blades of a helicopter lowering as it comes into land, wobbling as the wind force makes me a little unsteady on my feet. A door slides open.

"You may have won this time, Ella Jones, but you

haven't heard the last from me," Everett Croft bellows as the helicopter hovers loudly. "And River, you should know that no one betrays me and gets away with it. *No one!* Until we meet again!"

I hear the helicopter lift up and its door slide shut, before it turns, the beating blades speeding up and growing distant as it soars away across the city.

By the time we return to Everett's office, Finn tells me that Homados is awake but his hands are in chains, his head bowed as Lugh stands over where he's sitting.

"Everett Croft got away with it," Poppy glumly tells Lugh. "*Again*."

"There's not many places he can hide from me," Lugh responds, sounding almost amused. "Although getting involved in human affairs is frowned upon by the gods, I would be happy to step in to help you bring him to justice."

"I think after this experience I approve of the gods distancing themselves from human matters. Everett won't hide away forever. He likes the spotlight too much," I point out. "And it's not like we have any evidence that he was involved with the strange bouts of unbearable noise that the world has suffered."

"At least we've brought a stop to that," Finn

reasons. "I take it that, uh, Homados won't be trying it again any time soon?"

"Not much chance of that," Lugh assures us. "It would seem that the shield has already decided on how and what Homados should learn from his latest venture."

"I hope his headache lasts a long time," Poppy grumbles. "And you should keep those chains on him for as long as possible."

"I'm sorry to disappoint you, Poppy, but I only put those chains on him as a precaution while you were on the roof. Now that I have my spear back and Ella is here to pick up the shield, I'll release him."

Lugh mutters something and I hear the distinct clang of iron springing open before a sharp clattering as chains drop to the floor.

"Why are you letting him go?" River asks in horror, saying what we're all thinking.

"As I said, the shield has decided on how it should be," Lugh answers calmly.

"After all he tried to do, the shield sends him tumbling through the air and that's it? That's his punishment?" Finn checks, sounding very put out. "That noise was *excruciating*."

"When you left to chase after Everett Croft and

Homados awakened, I tried asking him a question and found he was unable to answer. He tried to speak to me, but he has become unable to say anything at all. Homados has lost his voice," Lugh explains.

"He had to speak aloud the incantations to create the noise of battle," I say. "Without his voice, he won't be able to do that."

"Rather humbling for the god of noise, don't you think?" Lugh comments. "Without his voice, Homados has lost the power he knew. The shield does not seek to punish, it hopes to educate. This is a new path for Homados and he will have to learn to adapt."

"I know a little bit about that," I say quietly.

Poppy takes my hand and squeezes it. "Sounds like Homados is about to embark on an adventure of his own. I hope he can do some serious soul searching. Oh, and Homados?" Poppy pauses, making sure she has his attention. "If ever you want to learn sign language, I might be able to give you some tips. Turns out I haven't forgotten all of it and it's thanks to you that I've remembered how beautiful a language it is."

Lugh chuckles softly. "And I should tell you, Homados, that after I beat the Machai you generously directed into my path, I secured their loyalty."

"The Mach-who?" Poppy asks.

"The Machai, spirits of battle in Greek mythology," Finn explains. "Powerful, terrifying daemons that you do *not* want to mess with."

"Should ever you get more ideas to encourage war among humans, Homados, you might want to think about how the Machai will greet you on my behalf," Lugh concludes.

Poppy lets go of my hand to bend down and pick up the shield, holding it out for me. "What are you going to do with this now, Ella? Mum and Dad will lose it when you bring this back. We could pretend you went to a cringe *Doctor Who* convention and bought this weird prop there."

"That's ridiculous," River says, unimpressed. "At least make it a *Warhammer* convention. More believable to buy a shield there I reckon."

"Ooh! We could have gone to a mythology convention!" Finn suggests excitedly. "I wonder if they exist. If they do, then Lugh, you should do a guest appearance! You would get a good reception, I promise. I could introduce you if you like."

"A generous offer," Lugh says, bemused.

"I won't be taking the shield home with me," I announce, to everyone's surprise. "I've decided that I should give it to you, Lugh. You came to us when we needed you, just like you promised, and you've shown Homados more mercy than he deserves." I take a step towards him and hold the shield up. "You and I had a bit of a rocky start, what with you stealing the light from the world and everything…"

There's a ripple of giggles from my friends, and even a chortle from Lugh himself.

"But we all make mistakes," I continue with a grin. "I know I can trust you."

"Thank you," he says, carefully lifting the shield from my grasp. "If you agree, then I would suggest we return the shield to Hercules in the Underworld, for it does belong to him. This, however, is yours."

Lugh mutters something under his breath, a spell I think, and I hear a *clunk*, like a machine being shut down. Moments later, he places the Eye of Horus back on its chain and into my palm. The sound I heard must have been him removing it from the shield.

"The shield will be incomplete, half its power with Hercules, half its power with you," he notes, as I gratefully return the pendant to hang round my neck. "Should anyone wish to use it, they'll have both of you to contend with."

"I don't fancy their chances," Poppy quips.

"Me neither," Lugh says lightly. "Now, it is

time for me to take my leave. Homados, you will accompany me. I believe Zeus would like to have a word."

"So you Celtic Greek gods just … hang out all together?" Finn asks, fascinated. "Are gods from other mythologies there? What do you even *talk* about?"

"This and that," Lugh replies warmly.

"Thank you for everything, Lugh," I say before Finn can bombard him with questions.

"It is an honour to stand beside you in battle, Ella Jones, whatever form that fighting may take," Lugh responds in a calm, resounding voice.

I hesitate. "Can I ask you for one more favour?"

"Anything."

"When we faced Medusa, one of our companions we met along the way was turned to stone. His name is Andrew. Do you know how we can save him and the others she's turned to stone? There has to be a way to turn them back."

"Leave that with me," Lugh says. "Medusa happens to owe me a favour. A story about a druid from a few centuries ago that I will tell you some other time."

"I bet you have the coolest stories," Finn mutters wistfully.

"I will make sure that your companion is no longer stone," Lugh promises.

I nod, beaming at him. "We won't have to wait for someone else to make a bid for unbeatable power over the human race before we meet you again, will we, Lugh?"

"I hope not. But, should anyone else have grand ideas to do so, at least the human race has five extraordinary heroes to protect it."

Maisie barks in response as if to say *Quite right!* and we all burst out laughing.

"Goodbye, Ella Jones," Lugh says, before I feel a *whoosh* of wind swirl round me.

I don't need the others to tell me that he and Homados are gone. You know when you're in the presence of a god and when you're not. I can sense that the glow from Lugh has vanished from the room.

"We should go," Poppy says as we hear sirens approaching the building. "I think breaking all the windows may have set off a few alarms."

"And I wouldn't put it past my uncle to have made some calls from the helicopter," River says with a heavy sigh. "I'm so sorry I lied to all of you. I wish I could go back in time and… Anyway, I understand if you don't want to talk to me ever again."

There's a beat of silence and I know Finn and Poppy are waiting for me to say something before they do. Maisie snorts impatiently, wondering why I'm taking so long. But I know how important this is and I want to make sure I say the right thing.

"River, you were only trying to make your family proud," I say gently. "Who's to say we wouldn't have done the same thing in your shoes? The important thing is that when you had to make a choice, you chose to do what's right instead of what's easy."

"Defying your uncle like that to give Ella the pendant was so brave," Finn jumps in.

"What kind of friends would we be if we didn't forgive you for trying to help your evil, villainous uncle in trying to take over the world?" Poppy says, prompting him to laugh.

I grin at him. "It's official. No way out. You're one of us now."

He sighs with relief. "I couldn't be happier about that."

"The thing is, River, when you save the world together, you form an unbreakable bond, no matter what comes your way next," Poppy declares, throwing her arm round my shoulders and pulling me close. "We speak from experience."

EPILOGUE

"I'm telling you –" Poppy says as she punches in the code to the gate and it swings open – "the chapters were brilliant, Ella. I'm so tired today because I couldn't stop reading last night. I couldn't put it down!"

I blush furiously as we walk across the gravel. "You're not just saying that to be nice?"

"When have I ever just said *anything* to be nice?" she says, balking at the suggestion.

"That's a fair point."

"She's not lying, Ella, your writing is so good," Finn agrees, strolling next to me. "I thought you told me you had writer's block."

"Not any more."

"Do you think that has something to do with

completing a quest created by Hermes and defeating the god of battle noise?" Finn says casually, prompting Poppy to snort. "Nothing like a good adventure to bring some inspiration."

"Actually, I don't think the inspiration came from the adventure itself," I tell him. "It was more to do with the people who accompanied me on it."

Maisie whines and huffs grumpily.

"And the dog too," I add hurriedly. "Maisie, you are my constant muse."

She snorts with satisfaction, and I can't help but giggle.

It's true that ever since we made our way down from Croft Tower and went home, I haven't been able to stop writing. It's as though the fog that was clouding my brain has lifted. Suddenly I have so much to say. In the last two weeks, around school and homework, I've been able to write several chapters of a fictional adventure book about some young unlikely heroes with a dash of mythology. I decided yesterday to let Poppy and Finn read what I'd written so far to get their opinion on how the first draft was shaping up.

The world has gradually started to relax now that there haven't been any further cases of the unbearable noise, although it's fair to say that everyone is a little shaken. With time, it will get better, and although no one understands what happened and Everett Croft remains at large without another blemish to his name, at least he'll know that Lugh will be keeping an eye on him. No matter how powerful a human you are, knowing a Celtic god isn't fooled by you is going to knock your confidence.

"You know what?" Poppy says. "It's much easier coming to River's house without having to climb over the wall."

I burst out laughing as we reach the end of his drive. "I can't believe you did that."

"Me neither," Finn says, stepping forward to ring the doorbell. "I'm surprised he's letting us come here again."

I smile warmly, excited to spend the day all together. Finn, Poppy and I have made a pact recently that whatever is going on in our lives – sports tournaments, zookeeping, mythological mysteries – we'll make time for each other. At the moment, we've committed to one evening a week or a weekend activity, which is why we put aside this Saturday morning to come to River's together.

"Just for the day, though, yes?" Dad called out

after us as we left the house earlier. "The last time you went to River's you stayed for a couple of days! If that happens again, I want calls and messages from you, not just from his butler. Poor guy needs a raise."

We promised we would call if that happened again.

But we're hoping it will be a while before Irving has to cover for us. We could all use a break from any mythological interventions. After our run-in with Homados, I took the chance to be honest with Poppy and Finn about how I'd been left feeling after the Day of Darkness: angry, confused, alone. Talking about it helped more than I could have imagined, and my honesty encouraged theirs. It turns out they'd been struggling too, but we'd managed it in different ways. Poppy had thrown herself into sports because exercise helped distract her from her fear of something like that happening again.

"If I talked about it, I was scared it would make it real," she admitted nervously. "It felt easier to pretend like nothing had ever happened."

"I think I've been using the zoo as a hideout," Finn said. "It was like I needed an escape from the world as I tried to process everything we'd been through."

After our open conversation, we realized that we'd

313

each felt that the rest of the world had forgotten and moved on without us. But all along, we hadn't been alone in that feeling.

This time, we've promised to talk about Homados and what happened in our own time, and we've been sure to tell River that he should do so, too.

"Homados has impressed upon me the importance of listening," Poppy remarked one evening earlier this week after she'd sent a message to our group WhatsApp to check in on how everyone was doing.

The group's title is currently *Lugh's Earthly Heroes*.

Finn changed it from the title Poppy had given it when she created the group with us and River, which was originally *Poppy vs The Mythological Dorks*.

"I'm glad Homados has taught you that. And how everyone deserves to have a voice," I added with a smile.

She took my hand and placed it over mine so she could sign to me: "No matter what."

A few seconds after Finn has pressed the bell, River's front door swings open.

"Hey, Irving!" Poppy cries, heading into the house before he can offer us the formal invitation. "How are you doing? Helped anyone break into any mansions lately?"

"I'm afraid I don't have any idea as to what you are talking about, Miss Jones," he replies deadpan, stepping aside as Maisie and I follow Poppy and Finn inside.

Once we left Croft Tower, River was able to get in contact with Irving at the hotel in Barra, who informed him that the fog had lifted. He was able to make travel arrangements to get home where he was forced to spend a few days resting his sprained ankle, a period of time neither he nor River were happy about. Irving is not a fan of sitting and doing nothing, and River kept catching him hobbling about the place, hoping to be useful. Apparently, they had a few "tense" conversations whenever River caught him and marched him back to his sofa where he proceeded to huff and mutter complaints under his breath.

In the end, River suggested he spend the time reading up on Greek mythology so he could teach River about it – funnily enough, River had a newfound appreciation for the subject. Irving was so thrilled at being given a task, he threw himself into it and studied as many books as possible, his foot elevated and rested the entire time.

Now, River says, Irving casually quotes mythological texts daily.

"May I offer you a beverage?" Irving asks us, closing the door.

"You may," Poppy says. "What have you got?"

"I can answer that," I say, jumping in quickly. "Everything. Whatever you can think of, Irving has it."

"In that case, please can you choose us something sparkling and *awesome*," Poppy directs. "Having witnessed the way you advised River on what to bring to rob Lord Almond, I'm going to trust your judgement."

"I have no recollection of a Lord Almond, Miss Jones, but I am delighted to have earned your trust and will endeavour to please in my selection," Irving says before he glides away.

"Hey, you're here!" River calls out from the floor above, and I hear him bound down the stairs, almost tripping over with excitement as he gets to the bottom few.

"We were reminiscing about our Lord Almond heist with Irving," Poppy jokes.

"Speaking of Lord Almond, did I tell you that he donated the map and compass to the Mythos Library?" I say, having received the call from Ailynn last night. "Apparently he said he felt something so amazing should be on public display – and also having them in his house gave him the creeps."

"Sensible guy," Poppy remarks. "So, River, what's the plan for today? You said on the group you had a surprise for us?"

"When I told Irving that you were all coming over this morning, he made some calls and all these video game companies sent us the coolest new games to try out. Some of them aren't even released yet! I don't know how Irving pulled this off, but I can't wait to try them."

"What?" Finn gasps. "That's amazing!"

"Irving is my hero," Poppy whispers. "He's like a mash up of James Bond and Jeeves."

"Come on," River says, leading us across the hall to a door at the far end. "Let's go to the games room. It's all set up in there."

"*Of course* you have a games room," Finn says, as we follow River who holds the door open for us and ushers us in. "Whoa! The screen is like … cinema size!"

"That's because it is cinema size," River admits modestly.

"This is amazing, thank you, River," Poppy says, clapping her hands. "These seats look comfortable." I hear her plonk herself down in one. "What game are we starting with?"

"I think Ella should pick," Finn declares, as I take off Maisie's harness so she can make herself comfortable. I hear Poppy encourage her to take the seat next to her.

"Here, Ella, I've laid them out for you on this table and they have Braille labels on them. These games are all accessible," River tells me.

"Thanks! Hmm. This is going to be a tough decision," I say, reading the titles.

"Choose your weapon wisely – I hear you're good at that," he says, chuckling softly.

"Hey Ella, I've just thought, you should send River your new chapters," Poppy suggests over the jangling of Maisie's collar as she gives her a good neck scratch.

"You've been writing your book?" River gasps excitedly. "How's it going so far?"

"It's been an adventure," I say, finally choosing a game for us to play and handing it to him with a wide grin. "But the story isn't finished yet."

ACKNOWLEDGEMENTS

Thank you to Ollie for running my businesses with me and always being my rock.

Katy Birchall, my wonderful co-author who puts up with my very detailed comments on Word. You are so talented and breathe life into the stories we write together.

Lauren Fortune and Olivia Towers, your constant support for Ella Jones as a series makes my heart happy. You both are the reason that visually impaired young people can see themselves represented on the Scholastic Book Fair shelves.

Lauren Gardner and Callen Martin, my literary agents who have been there from the beginning of my book journey. Thank you for always believing in me.

Last, but certainly not least, Katrina, Ella and the 84 World team. You're all always by my side through the highs and the lows and I'm so happy and lucky to share this high with you all.

Katy Birchall is the author of several young adult and teen novels, including *The It Girl* series, the *Hotel Royale* series and *Morgan Charmley: Teen Witch*. She is the co-author, with Alesha Dixon, of the middle-grade *Lightning Girl* series, *Star Switch*, *Girls Rule* and the *Luna Wolf* books, plus a retelling of Jane Austen's *Emma* for the *Awesomely Austen* series and *Sex Education: The Road Trip*. She is also the author of several romantic comedies including *The Secret Bridesmaid*, *The Wedding Season* and *The Last Word*, and writes romantic sports fiction for young adults under the name Ivy Bailey. Katy lives in London with her partner, daughter and rescue dog.

Have you read the first Ella Jones adventure?

When Ella visits central London with her family, a light
in the world is suddenly extinguished, causing panic and
chaos as people are plunged into pitch black. A pagan god
of light, Lugh, has been released from his millennium-old
prison by a shadowy villain and, out for revenge on humans,
has brought darkness down on the world.

Ella, though, is the hero the world needs.
Used to living her life in darkness every day,
can she keep calm and work out a plan to defeat
Lugh and return light to the world?